As they neared the perp's sedan, heavy thuds sounded from the trunk.

Trey closed his K-9 partner's divider, then he withdrew his weapon and inched closer.

The thudding increased.

Carefully, Trey released the trunk and stepped back, gun at the ready.

A woman lay faceup, arms and ankles bound. She jerked awkwardly, trying to kick him, desperation in each movement. Muffled screams indicated she was gagged under the black hood covering her head.

"Ma'am, my name is Trooper Jackson. I'm here to help you. You're safe."

She stopped flailing, her frame rigid.

"I'm going to remove the hood."

Trey leaned in, gently pulling the fabric free.

She wrenched back. Dark tendrils streaked her face and her wide hazel eyes pierced him, terror written on her expression.

Several seconds ticked by as he absorbed the sight.

Finally, he found his voice. "Justine Stark, is that you?"

Sharee Stover is a Colorado native transplanted to Nebraska, where she lives with her husband, three children and two dogs. Her mother instilled in her a love of books before Sharee could read, along with the promise "If you can read, you can do anything." When she's not writing, she enjoys time with her family, long walks with her obnoxiously lovable German shepherd and crocheting. Find her at shareestover.com or on Twitter, @shareestover.

Books by Sharee Stover

Love Inspired Suspense

Secret Past
Silent Night Suspect
Untraceable Evidence
Grave Christmas Secrets
Cold Case Trail

Visit the Author Profile page at Harlequin.com.

COLD CASE TRAIL

SHAREE STOVER

LOVE INSPIRED SUSPENSE

INSPIRATIONAL ROMANCE

LOVE INSPIRED SUSPENSE
INSPIRATIONAL ROMANCE

ISBN-13: 978-1-335-72243-0

Recycling programs for this product may not exist in your area.

Cold Case Trail

This edition published by arrangement with Harlequin Books S.A.

For questions and comments about the quality of this book, please contact us at CustomerService@Harlequin.com.

Love Inspired
22 Adelaide St. West, 40th Floor
Toronto, Ontario M5H 4E3, Canada
www.Harlequin.com

Printed in U.S.A.

And ye shall know the truth,
and the truth shall make you free.
–John 8:32

For my daughter, Andi. Your love for K-9s and their law enforcement handlers inspired Magnum's story.

Many thanks to:

My amazing editor, Emily Rodmell, for her encouragement and support.

Trooper Levi Cockle and K-9 Cole for their expertise and service.

ONE

He's been in my apartment, I'm sure of it. Is he watching me now?

Forensic psychologist Justine Stark glanced over her shoulder and shivered. A slight breeze rustled the oak tree leaves near the pasture, and the wind chime overhead sang softly. She searched for movement in the inky night but spotted nothing out of the ordinary. Her surroundings stilled, and she returned her attention to the diary's worn brown leather cover. Somewhere within its pages, she'd decipher the clues to develop a criminal profile to catch the killer.

First, she had to compartmentalize her emotions, a liability for any investigation. Except her throat tightened at the sight of her best friend's flamboyant handwriting, as whimsical as the woman who'd penned the contents. Worse, Justine almost heard Kayla Nolan's terrified voice in each entry, even a decade after her death.

Justine wrapped herself in a hug, warding off the chill, though the summer air was balmy. Slowing the old porch swing, she noted Kayla's fear escalation and stalker-related entries. The shrill ring of her cell phone sent her pen skidding off the paper.

A nervous chuckle escaped, and she glanced at the screen. Caller Unknown. Was the Nebraska State Patrol investigator in charge of Kayla's case finally returning her call? Or had Harry Dante found time to harass her from prison again?

A second ring. She contemplated letting it go to voice mail, except she wanted to talk to the investigator. "Hello?"

Silence, then heavy breathing.

Her irritation increased. "Give it up, Harry."

A responding dial tone.

She sighed and set the phone atop the notebook. Her extensive profiling and criminal-trial testimonies produced a growing list of haters, but dealing with the harassment never got easier.

Dante had sworn revenge on everyone involved in his sentencing hearing. Over the past year, he'd bombarded Justine with not-so-anonymous hate mail and a steady stream of untraceable calls. Certain Dante used a burner phone, she'd contacted the warden. He'd disregarded the claim, stating prisoners had access only to landlines.

Changing her number had proved futile because the calls continued. The final straw—the vandalism of her car outside her Lincoln apartment—prompted her relocation three hours away to the rural twelve-acre, fixer-upper ranch in the far northeastern part of Nebraska.

Justine resumed swaying, focused on the abundance of fireflies dancing in the night sky to the cadence of crickets and cicadas. The sweet scent of lilacs wafted from the overgrown bushes bordering the two-story farmhouse wraparound porch, calming her.

You're safe here. She rehearsed the comforting mantra, relishing the haven where she fostered dogs for the overflowing animal shelter in town.

Lifting the diary again, Justine angled the page, allowing her to read by the soft glow of the porch light. She donned the persona of a clinician, shoving aside the guilt-ridden heart she had for failing to save her best friend.

Kayla's scribblings testified to a nameless, faceless psychopath, who'd tormented her by leaving bizarre gifts inside her apartment. Though she'd tried to report the incidents, no one except Justine had believed her. The authorities had classified Kayla's death as suspicious, claiming it was an overdose after a drug buy gone bad. And they were wrong because Justine knew her friend never used drugs. Kayla had been murdered. But why?

What she hadn't done ten years ago, she'd accomplish now and ensure Kayla got justice. The diary was a beginning, but Justine wanted the investigator's evidence files, even if it meant storming his office door.

Clover stretched out a reassuring paw before consuming the rest of the porch swing with her furry body.

"Am I in your way?" Justine ruffled the overweight calico's velvety fur.

Sharp, piercing barks emitted from the renovated

barn, sending Justine's pulse racing. She placed a hand over her chest. "I'd better go to bed before every noise gives me a heart attack. What is going on with the boys?"

Clover yawned, indifferent to the commotion.

"Thanks for your support," Justine teased, pushing off the swing. She stepped down to the lawn and rounded the house, aiming for the barn—affectionately dubbed the Dog House—with Clover accompanying her.

An ambient glow stretched from the building's ajar door, slowing Justine. Hadn't she locked up after feeding the boys?

Uneasiness crept between her shoulders. She paused, turned and scanned the surrounding trees, casting shadows with their canopy of leaves.

You're safe here.

The dogs continued barking in an uneven banter.

A rustle sent the calico darting off, startling Justine. "Stop that," she admonished herself.

Too bad Clover wasn't an attack cat.

Should she enter? And what other choice did she have? Mr. Richardson, her closest neighbor, lived a half mile adjacent from her. The unpleasant man was more interested in taking ownership of her property rather than helping her.

Justine still clutched the diary. She shoved it into the large pocket of her khaki cargo shorts. Inhaling a fortifying breath, she pushed wide the door and, in a single stride, stepped inside and flipped on the overhead lights. "Gentlemen, what's with all the hullabaloo?"

At her entrance, the barking ceased and five tails wagged in greeting. A quick scan confirmed an empty room, except for the motley crew of mutts. Justine studied the door, accepting she'd earlier failed to close it properly.

Or a raccoon got in, explaining Clover's sudden departure. The varmints had discovered the building held an abundance of food, making them a recent nuisance.

"It's bedtime." Talking to the dogs calmed her.

Justine double-checked each kennel and resident, providing a few minutes of attention.

She saved the neediest patient for last. "Hey, Barney, how're you feeling?" Justine knelt beside the senior basset hound recovering from a broken leg.

He gave her a rhythmic thump of his tail while lounging on his doggie cot, his big brown eyes pleading.

"I promise you'll return to the house once you're able to climb the stairs again."

Barney harrumphed and laid his head down, dangling his long ears over the edge.

She chuckled and exited the kennel, giving the space one last perusal. A countertop on the far side, along with a sink and cabinets, held the dogs' food, treats and medications. Her part-time ranch hand's accommodations were cordoned off on the right. The barn was spotless, and since the installation of the air conditioner, the temperature remained comfortable.

Next year she'd install the same amenities in the old farmhouse, but that was a luxury she'd have to save up for. Barney's unexpected arrival and medical treatment, the renovations for the Dog House, along with canine flea and tick medications, had consumed this year's funds.

"That's enough ruckus for one night. Go to sleep and I'll see you tomorrow." She exited the building and pulled the door shut.

From the shadows, Clover reappeared.

"Did you chase off the raccoon?"

The calico's tail stood tall as they traversed back to the house.

Will Percy, her hired hand, would arrive in the morning. He worked hard, but his busy schedule and her lack of money made his assistance sporadic at best. There was never enough time, cash or able-bodied help to keep up with the ranch. Dreams might tarry, but she'd invested everything to breathe life into hers.

Her shoes thudded against the rotting porch wood as she rounded the house. Gathering her notes and phone from the swing, she tugged open the rickety screen door. A wave of humidity and stuffy air spilled out, and the grandfather clock chimed ten o'clock from the corner of the living room. After flipping on every light between the entrance and the kitchen, she determined to read the diary a half hour longer before going to bed.

The lights flickered, then went out, thrusting Justine into pitch-dark. She pivoted on one foot, eyes focused on the door. Probably just needed to reset the fuse box.

In the basement.

A lump formed in her throat. "Clover?" Justine squeaked, hating the quiver in her voice. "Here, kitty-kitty."

Because the cat could reset the fuse box? Were raccoons responsible for the blackout? Doubtful. The hundred-year-old house offered a variety of creepy noises, and functional errors happened occasionally.

You're safe here.

Why hadn't she brought Barney inside? Perhaps calling for help would be wiser. And say what? *My lights went out, and I'm a big baby and don't want to go into the basement by myself*?

Justine threw back her shoulders and stood taller. No, this was just another part of living in the country as an independent woman.

Inching across the kitchen, she felt her way to the junk drawer and groped for a flashlight. At last, her hands gripped the cold metal, bringing a small measure of comfort. She flipped the switch, exhaling relief at the responsive beam.

"You are always with me, Lord."

A resounding meow blazed a voltage through her heart, and she laughed nervously.

"Clover, you about shot me through the roof." Justine wedged the flashlight under her armpit and lifted the cat, stroking her fur.

The knife block beside her had Justine considering her options.

"Stop that."

Clover fidgeted, forcing Justine to set her down.

"Sorry, not you." She snagged a butcher knife and, gripping the flashlight, made her way through the kitchen. "Nothing but a blown fuse. Get a grip."

Her footsteps echoed on the creaky floors—a multifunctional feature, making the home endearing in the daylight and eerie at night. She tugged the basement door open, releasing dank mustiness into the hallway.

Justine reached in and flipped on the light switch, hoping against reality it worked.

Nope.

She swiped her clammy palm on her shirt, readjusted the flashlight in her left hand and clutched the knife in her right. Justine descended the steep cement steps, trying hard not to think about the encroaching darkness. A wisp of something grazed her face. She swatted away the sticky substance, but the spiderweb remnants clung to her skin. Justine shook them off and wiped her hand on her pant leg.

At the bottom of the steps, she inhaled and swung the beam, illuminating the fuse box. Destination in sight, she sprinted for the corner of the cinder block basement and reached for the metal door.

A shadow shifted in her peripheral vision.

Justine spun, her nose connecting with someone's fist. The force thrust her into the wall.

The flashlight toppled to the cement floor with a thud before dying.

Grasping the knife, Justine screamed a battle cry, flailing the blade blindly around her. She kicked in every direction and a resounding "oomph" from the invader confirmed she'd made a connection.

Justine fought, slashing the knife in front of her, unrelenting. Though he never spoke, her attacker's labored breathing echoed around her.

Then everything stilled.

Had he fled? She squatted, groping for the flashlight.

Her fingertips touched the cold metal.

A tackle from behind flattened Justine against the cement floor, jolting the knife from her hand.

The intruder restrained her wrists behind her back and secured bindings on her ankles.

"Where is it?" he growled.

Did he know about Kayla's diary? Had he watched Justine reading? She swallowed. The weight of the small book in her pocket anchored her.

"What are you talking about?"

"Fine. We'll do this the hard way." He slapped tape over her mouth, restricting breathing to her nose, and covered her head with a hood.

Lord, what's happening? Help me!

Strong arms gripped, lifted and inverted her, gravity rushing blood to her brain. He ascended the stairs. Heavy footsteps reverberated on the wood floor, indicating they were in the hallway. Justine forced herself to focus on the details. She'd need them to escape. Hysteria wouldn't help. If there was ever a time to lean on her psychology training, it was now. She'd outwit the perpetrator and flee. Somehow.

He crossed the living room and descended the porch steps. How had he gotten to the ranch? She'd have seen him driving up to the property. Had he waited by the Dog House? Was that what had riled the boys?

She bounced against his shoulder, nausea building.

The man paused.

Justine squirmed to break free, helpless against his tightening hold.

"Knock it off."

A familiar beep, like a key fob release. In a swoop, he dropped her, and she landed with a hard thud. Rough material brushed against her arms and legs. Carpet. She was in a trunk.

A slam, and his footsteps faded.

Justine calmed her breathing to combat the panic of the smothering tape and hood. She tugged against the restraints and tried scooting out of the hood, using the carpet.

To no avail.

Several long minutes passed. What was he doing? Would he kill her?

Finally, a second slam and the engine roared to life. Justine sniffed, inhaling the bitter scent of fertilizer. She'd loaded the bags earlier in the day. He was using her car to kidnap her.

The vehicle reversed.

Justine focused on the details. She'd find her way home once she escaped her bindings.

He shifted again and drove forward, leaving her property. The connecting dirt road was rough. If the man was a local or if he'd cased her place, he'd be aware of the large pothole left over from the last major flood.

She braced, waiting. Sure enough, the car dipped into the rut, slamming her face into the floor. A blast of pain coursed through her nose. Not a local. She made the mental note, beginning her depiction tactics. She didn't need to see his face to create a profile. He would not get away with this.

Justine shifted to her back, with the coordination of a wounded caterpillar. The vehicle slowed, rolling her to the side. He'd turned left onto the major county highway, heading east.

If she freed her hands, she'd grasp the trunk release. Every car had one, or so she'd read.

Justine tugged her arms apart, trying to break through the zip ties. She kicked, extending her efforts there, but the plastic tore at the tender skin around her ankles.

The car accelerated.

Lord, please get me out of this!

Nebraska state trooper Trey Jackson was about to walk into an ambush. The perfect ending to the worst day ever. And he'd chosen it willingly. As if postponing his K-9 partner Magnum's recertification exam wasn't bad enough, his nemesis, Eric Irwin, had offered to fill their spot in the meantime. Thankfully, Sergeant Oliver had declined, but not before warning Trey their assigned work area needed a capable K-9 team soon. To top it off, Justine Stark would slam the door in his face when he arrived unannounced at her house in less than ten minutes.

She detested Trey.

Rightfully so, after he'd failed to respond to their mutual friend Kayla Nolan the night of her murder. He should've been the first to arrive at her apartment. No excuses. Still, he wished Justine had allowed him to explain.

Kayla was high-strung and openly communicated her feelings for Trey to anyone who would listen. He hadn't reciprocated, and finally confessed he was interested in Justine. Kayla refused to accept that fact. Trey assumed Kayla had told Justine how he felt, especially when the trio's friendship grew tense shortly thereafter. He interpreted the change as Justine's rejection of him. Still, Kayla never gave up on trying to win him over.

The night Kayla called with wild claims of a stalker, Trey and Magnum were working their first manhunt. Unable to leave, Trey sent his brother and fellow trooper, Slade, in his place. But when Kayla saw Slade, she slammed the door in his face.

Trey's reasons for not showing up that night might've seemed justifiable from the outside, but he willingly bore Justine's disdain along with his own guilt.

He allowed his thoughts to return to Irwin, not wanting to consider the possible outcomes with Justine yet.

Trey was all for healthy competition, but Irwin played on his anxiety. A forced recovery risked re-injuring Magnum. Not an option. Regardless of his insecurities over the possibility of losing their position. Grip tightening on the steering wheel, Trey pictured the last interaction with Irwin.

"Magnum's past his prime. You should retire him," the younger trooper had commented.

A new wave of irritation flowed through him. "Over my dead body," Trey grunted, feeling the urge to slug Irwin's smug face the next time he saw the man.

The Belgian Malinois whined from his temperature-controlled space and poked his triangular head through the truck's divider.

Trey reached up and scratched his scruff. "Sorry, boy. Thinking about Irwin."

Magnum gave a sympathetic and well-timed bark of understanding.

"See, you totally get it." Trey rewarded him with a good ear scratching. "But Oliver thinks he's Mr. Helpful. More like a vulture circling its prey."

Magnum rested his head on Trey's shoulder.

"Don't worry, buddy. You're healing fine, and we'll be back in the saddle. Right now, though, I need a little courage to handle the blast from my past. You know, this could go really bad. I mean, worst-case scenario, Justine slams the door in my face. Hopefully, we'll get the best-case scenario and she'll hear me out once she sees the files I brought."

Almost ten years had passed since their last interaction, and that hadn't been pleasant. They'd scarcely spoken at Kayla's funeral, and the death daggers Justine had shot from across the room were enough to kill.

Sergeant Oliver hadn't forbidden Trey to make the long commute to Justine's home, though his disapproval at the personal visit hadn't gone unnoticed.

"What choice do I have, Mags? If I'd called first, Justine would've hung up as soon as I said my name. She hates me."

And he deserved it. If he'd been there for Kayla, she'd be alive.

Trey glanced at the cold-case file box riding shotgun beside him, contemplating for the hundredth time if this was the wisest action. Were Kayla's files enough incentive for Justine to listen to him?

The shorter and less painful option was a phone call.

And cowardly.

The face-to-face meeting was his one chance to right the wrong. However pitiful the step might be. "Let's pray for the best."

Magnum sighed and slipped back into his space.

"Thanks for the reassurance."

Trey's phone rang.

"Call from Sergeant Oliver," the automated voice announced.

Trey answered using his hands-free device. "Boss."

"Where are you?"

"Almost to the Stark residence, if Callista correctly recorded the address." The patrol secretary, Callista Neff, was knowledgeable and a valuable asset. However, her attention to detail and customer service skills ebbed and flowed depending on her mood of the day.

"Jackson, you should've returned her call." His placating tone reemphasized disapproval, but Oliver wasn't privy to Trey and Justine's history, and he didn't need the details.

"No worries, Sarge. Magnum and I wanted to get out of the office anyway."

"Understood. Besides, after the way Callista

treated Miss Stark, it's probably not a bad idea to do some damage control."

"Ouch."

Oliver grunted. "Yeah, I only heard half the conversation, but it was less than cordial. Monday, I'll be meeting with Callista about her attitude. Again."

"Those are becoming a regular occurrence."

"Don't remind me. I'm headed to the lake for the weekend, but let me know if Miss Stark provides any leads. Although after—what?—nine, no, ten years, I seriously doubt she'll have anything to offer."

"Except she's a highly qualified forensic psychologist now. The patrol didn't pursue criminal profiling back then. Maybe her skills will help us solve Kayla Nolan's case."

"You don't have to sell me on the idea. That's my hope, Jackson."

Tension lessened in Trey's shoulders. His boss's support bolstered his confidence.

"How's Magnum doing? I assume he's enjoying the ride along with you?"

"He's eating up the attention and relaxing. I considered leaving him behind, but the last time he got depressed. He likes working, even if it's not to his full capacity."

Oliver chuckled. "I appreciate a dog's need to be useful, but watch that he doesn't reinjure his paw. You've only got two weeks until the next K-9 recertification."

As if Trey needed the reminder. "Roger that. Thanks again for letting us work cold cases."

"It's the least we can do for him," Oliver replied. "If he needs more time, Eric—"

"Mags will be healed in time, boss." Trey cringed at the rude interruption, but the last thing he wanted was another rendition of Eric the Vulture's brilliant and magnificent capability. "We'll make our recert."

"I have no doubt."

"Thanks."

They disconnected, and Trey exhaled relief. Magnum was getting into his senior years, but he was far from retirement. They were in their prime, a solid team with the highest takedowns, manhunt recoveries and drug interdictions. At least, they had been. On their last case, Magnum cut his front paw on debris in the sewer tunnel where the subject was hiding.

Be anxious for nothing. The soft reminder floated in Trey's mind. "You're right, Lord. Worrying won't solve anything. You've got this case, and You've got us."

The automated GPS voice advised Trey to take a left in a mile. He crested the hill and was blinded by oncoming headlights. The vehicle sped in Trey's lane, swerving at the last minute to avoid a head-on collision, then whipped past, accelerating.

"I don't think so, dude." Trey flipped on his sirens and lights and made a U-turn, pursuing. He closed the distance to read the license plate and radioed in the information.

The sedan skidded around the corner, merging onto the highway.

"You're seriously trying to outrun me?"

As if the driver heard Trey, the car slowed, right-turn signal blinking as he edged to the shoulder.

"What an idiot. Drive out to the highway, where there's traffic, instead of stopping on the safety of the side road?" Trey mumbled. Whatever. This guy had earned a ticket tonight. "Well, that was uneventful." He pulled behind the sedan, deactivated the siren, but left his overhead lights swirling to warn oncoming traffic.

Trey grabbed his uniform hat, placing it on his head, and collected his flashlight. "Five-five-nine-nine, 10-82," he spoke into the radio, notifying the dispatcher of his badge number and the ten code for pulling over a vehicle.

A couple of cars heading westbound passed, and Trey waited until it was clear to exit the pickup. Flashlight on, he approached the sedan's passenger side. A change in recent years after multitudes of officers were struck by motorists during routine stops. He watched the driver for any sudden movements.

One occupant. Probably a texting-and-driving situation—another development responsible for accidents lately. The front passenger-side window lowered.

Trey leaned closer. "Good eve—" His intro was cut off as the driver lifted a gun and aimed it in his direction.

Trey dropped and flattened against the gravel road, reaching for his weapon.

"Plates are registered to—" Gunfire exploded, drowning out the dispatcher's voice in his earpiece.

"Shots fired! Shots fired!" Trey hollered into his shoulder mic, simultaneously army crawling backward and staying low to the ground.

Once he reached the safety of the vehicle's quarter panel, he glanced up and returned fire, then ducked again.

Headlights beamed from an oncoming SUV, cresting the hill. If he didn't get control of the situation, an innocent passerby might be killed.

A long silence motivated Trey to peer around the car.

The driver ran from the sedan, turned and fired, then bolted for the SUV, waving down the motorist.

Trey sprinted after him.

Too late. The driver stopped, and the shooter flung open the door, yanking out an elderly man who rolled helplessly onto the highway. The subject sped away in the stolen truck.

"Sir, are you okay?" Trey helped the victim to his feet.

"I don't know what happened," he said, weaving unsteadily.

"What's your name?"

"Edwin Smith."

On the way to his patrol vehicle, Trey collected information from Mr. Smith and called in the carjacking, issuing a BOLO—be on the lookout—for the subject. The criminal couldn't outrun the radio.

As they neared the sedan, heavy thuds sounded from the trunk. Trey ran to his pickup and closed Magnum's divider, then waved over Mr. Smith. "Please wait inside for me."

Trey withdrew his weapon and inched closer to the car.

The thudding increased.

Carefully, Trey released the trunk and stepped back, gun at the ready.

A woman lay faceup, arms tucked under her and ankles bound. She jerked awkwardly, trying to kick him, desperation in each movement. Muffled screams indicated she was gagged under the black hood covering her head.

"Ma'am, my name is Trooper Jackson. I'm here to help you. You're safe."

She stopped flailing, her frame rigid.

"I'm going to remove the hood."

Trey leaned in, gently pulling the fabric free, over her head.

She wrenched back. Dark tendrils streaked her face, and her wide hazel eyes pierced him, terror written on her expression.

Several seconds ticked by as he absorbed the sight.

Finally, he found his voice. "Justine Stark, is that you?"

TWO

Justine blinked, then attempted to answer, only to find her words stuck in the tape covering her mouth.

"I'll rip off the tape, but it'll sting."

She braced, and true to Trey's warning, the tape didn't disappoint. Justine inhaled, filling her lungs with fresh air. "Thank you. I heard gunshots. Is he—?" She didn't finish the sentence, allowing her gaze to search for the kidnapper.

He sliced through her bindings, then helped her out of the trunk.

"I planned to meet at your house, but I guess this works," he quipped, flashing a dimple in his smile.

Justine's expression must've spoken questions and disapproval, because he quickly sobered.

"Why were you coming to my home?" She spun, searching. "Did you arrest the man who kidnapped me?"

A small wince crossed Trey's face. "No. He carjacked Mr. Smith's vehicle and got away."

He gestured to a patrol K-9 pickup behind them, with strobing red-and-blue lights. An elderly man sat in the passenger seat, his mouth set in an O shape.

"But I have a BOLO out for the subject," Trey added. "We'll get his identity from the registration on this—"

"It's my car," Justine inserted.

He did a double take. "He used your car to kid-nap you?"

"Yes."

"Are you okay? I'll call for an ambulance." Trey reached for his shoulder mic.

Justine shook her head. "I'm fine. Really." Un-true, but she didn't need medical care or the ac-companying expense. Her hand brushed the pocket containing the diary. For a millisecond, she consid-ered telling Trey about the evidence, then decided against it. Not until she'd spoken with the case in-vestigator.

Trey held out a notepad. "Can you identify the subject?"

"Nope. One minute, I'm in my house, trying to reset the fuse box. The next, I'm in the trunk of my car, fighting for my life." Justine wrapped herself in a hug, warding off the chill that had nothing to do with the temperature and everything to do with the terror she'd encountered.

A second patrol vehicle pulled up, contributing to the strobing lights.

"Give me a second while I ask the trooper to take Mr. Smith's statement. Then I'll drive you home. We'll have your car towed back." He rushed off without giving her a chance to respond.

Justine walked to the driver's side, slid behind the wheel and adjusted the seat. The familiar road sign ahead assured her they hadn't driven far from her ranch.

Trey appeared at her window. "Planning on racing off?"

She glanced up. "The perp was much taller than me. Easily over six feet, based on where the seat was when I got in."

"That helps." He withdrew a notepad and marked down the information. "You might be surprised what details you remember when we do the report."

She stifled her groan. He needed a full accounting of the event, and though she'd never admit it to him, the thought of returning to her ranch alone was a little disconcerting. The dogs! Had the kidnapper hurt them? "My boys! I have to go home. Now!"

Trey's eyes widened. "Your boys?"

She started the engine.

"Are you sure you're okay to drive? You're still shook up."

"I'm fine." Why did everything she say come out so harshly? Because being in Trey's presence was unnerving. "I appreciate the offer though," she added, nearly whacking him with the door as she pulled it closed.

"I'll follow you, then."

Justine waited for him to reach his pickup before she merged onto the road. He slipped behind her, sans strobing lights.

What was Trey doing in this part of the state? Not that she kept tabs on him, but the law enforcement circles were small. There was no denying the one advantage of Trey's unexpected return to her life was his access to Kayla's case files. She'd insist on his help and wouldn't take no for an answer.

He owed her.

No. He owed Kayla. Trey and Justine were Kayla's closest friends. When she'd called him that night, claiming someone was stalking her, Trey hadn't bothered showing up. But then, neither had Justine.

The thought was an arrow to her heart. No. That was different. Justine had been out of town. Besides, Kayla had made it clear—she only wanted Trey's help. She'd laid claim to Trey early on, eliminating any opportunity for Justine to share how she felt about him.

Just as well. He'd failed Kayla when she needed him most. Like Justine's ex Simon, who'd betrayed and stolen from her. Proof that letting down her guard was unwise. Justine pushed aside the unwelcome thoughts, returning to Kayla.

The night replayed in her mind, an endless spooling reel of Kayla's frantic phone call. They'd talked into the early morning hours, Justine refusing to hang up until Kayla de-escalated. She'd rambled on about her feelings for Trey. Justine chalked up the hysteria of his nonarrival to her friend's theatrics. Especially after Kayla apologized and said she'd gotten scared over nothing.

That was the last time they'd spoken. Two days later, Justine returned to Lincoln. She'd driven from the airport straight to Kayla's apartment, only to find it cordoned off with police tape. She hadn't spoken to Trey since Kayla's funeral. It had been all too raw that day. But a decade was a long time.

Refocusing her energy, Justine processed the questions barreling full speed at her.

Why would someone kidnap her? In her own car?

She gripped the steering wheel. "Thank You, Lord, for rescuing me. Although, for the record, You could've chosen someone else. Your ways, not mine. I need Your help. Kayla deserves justice."

As she neared Vincent Richardson's ranch—her only neighbor and a cantankerous man she'd nicknamed Mr. Personality—she slowed, searching for a vehicle. Richardson's cows meandered the perimeter, and the house was hidden beneath a canopy of mature trees. She'd contact him in the morning and ask if he'd seen anyone lurking around her property. Mr. Personality's less-than-cordial attitude made the possibility of a stranger parking his pre-kidnapping vehicle on his land improbable.

Had the perp watched her? Justine replayed Kayla's words about a stalker and shuddered as she pulled into the detached two-car garage, triggering the motion-sensor lights.

Trey parked behind her, blocking her in. Annoyed but focused on the boys, she exited the car and headed for the barn. Most likely, the kidnapper hadn't bothered the dogs, but she'd feel better after confirming that with her own eyes.

Trey started toward the darkened farmhouse as

she hurried past him to the barn. "Wait. Where are you going?"

She waved him over. "In there."

He hurried to her side, confusion etched in his blue eyes. "Your children are alone in a barn?"

That brought a laugh to her lips. "Sort of. Foster dogs." She pulled open the door, welcomed by a rendition of barks. Justine led him through the building, releasing each dog from their kennels. "There are five males, so I refer to them as the boys."

In a tail-wagging flurry, the canines rushed to greet the newcomer. He gave each one attention, and she marveled at the ease in Trey's demeanor. Did he have to be great with animals? It was getting harder to maintain her animosity.

Trey moved slowly around the perimeter and seemed to linger at Will's meager accommodations. A large section of plywood separated the mini living quarters furnished with a twin bed, table and light. She started to explain, then reconsidered. Trey didn't need information about her life.

He crossed the room to her. "Are they okay with outsider dogs?"

"Yep. We're working on socialization, and it's gone well."

"In that case, I'll release my partner. He could use a bathroom break."

She did a double take deciphering his request. She followed him out, the boys bounding along.

Trey jogged to his truck and opened the back

door. He turned, cradling a Belgian Malinois with a gauze-wrapped right front paw.

Justine's heart melted against her stony exterior. "Aw, what happened to him?" Her feet rushed forward against her brain's reservations.

"Magnum cut his paw on a manhunt. He's healing ahead of schedule though." Trey gently steadied the dog on his three good legs. "Where can he use your, uh, facilities?"

She pointed to the grassy area beside the garage, where two of the boys sniffed the ground.

"May I pet him?" She reached out, then quickly retracted her arm. "Sorry, never mind. Police dogs aren't allowed to socialize."

Trey laughed. "Magnum never received that memo. However, he's got intuition like no other. He can sniff out a criminal in an auditorium filled with people. I must warn you, he's a horrible flirt."

Much like his master. Justine stifled her reply and squatted. Magnum hobbled to her and dropped to a sit. She allowed him to sniff her hands. Then, at his approval, she petted his soft fur. "He's beautiful."

"And he knows it."

So incredibly not fair. She could've resisted handcuffs, demands, even a hostage negotiator, but Trey used the ultimate incentive. An adorable and wounded animal. For that, she had no defense.

"He doesn't mind other dogs?"

"Not unless they're breaking the law."

"My boys are legal, just in need of a little rehab. I'm grateful that creep didn't hurt them."

"Aren't you worried they'll run off?"

"This is Club Med for them, probably the best life any of them have known." The dogs' sorrowful histories gave her pause. Part of the reason she labored and sacrificed for them. "Their electric collars and underground fencing keep them quarantined on the premises, allowing them to run freely without leashes. No escape attempts yet."

"You live here alone?"

"Yep." She stepped away, avoiding the conversation.

Her heart bubbled with love for the canines frolicking on the ranch. Between the bounty of repairs, never-ending projects, and her consulting and expert-testimony schedule, Justine was too busy to bemoan her nonexistent love life, not that she'd give another man her heart. Instead, she lavished attention on the only creatures worthy and capable of unconditional love. In turn, they never judged her by the scars on her heart or body.

At the reminder, Justine tugged down her sleeves and whistled for the boys. "Give me a sec."

Magnum moved to Trey's side. "Need help?"

"No, this is our routine." Justine finished securing each dog and locking the building, then walked to Trey.

"That didn't take long."

"Nope, got it down to a fine art." She swatted a

persistent mosquito. "Let's go inside. There's no air-conditioning, but we won't become dinner for the local insect population."

He lingered before following her. "What happened before the kidnapping?"

"The boys were riled up, and the Dog House door was ajar."

"Was that strange? Do you leave it open?"

Justine led the way across the property, with Magnum and Trey keeping pace. "The barn's temperature controlled, so I keep the door shut. Especially with the recent raccoon invasions. Clover tore after something, and I assumed she chased a raccoon. The boys were fine, so I locked up and headed into the house."

"Clover?"

"My cat." Justine gazed out toward the pasture. "She's around somewhere."

When they reached the porch, Trey carried Magnum up the steps. "This place is nice. Reminds me of my folks' house."

"Needs work, but I love it."

"Mom and Pops would make homemade ice cream—they came up with wild combinations—and we'd spend summer evenings eating their latest concoctions on their wraparound porch, playing games and singing horribly out-of-tune songs."

Justine remained silent at Trey's wistful comment. What must it be like to have a loving family connection? She'd never know. Her fingers traced the burn scars on her upper arm—hidden, like her painful and embarrassing past—beneath the long-sleeved thin cotton shirt.

A twinge of jealousy niggled, but the solid reminder of who she was and what she needed to do for Kayla refocused her thoughts. She and Trey weren't friends hanging out and socializing. They existed in different worlds. Once he took her statement, he'd be out of her life.

Justine's front door stood open, exposing the darkened rooms inside, her haven no longer. "Guess locking up before he abducted me was too much to ask," she said sarcastically.

The roar of an engine interrupted them. Headlights beamed from the county road. A lifted diesel dually turned onto her property, almost taking out her fence.

"Are you expecting someone?"

"No." Was the kidnapper returning? Certainly not with a cop there. Except Trey's patrol vehicle wasn't visible from the oncoming truck's view.

Trey withdrew his gun and stepped in front of her. "Go inside and lock the door. Call for help if this goes bad. Magnum stay." He descended the porch, gun in hand.

The truck accelerated, kicking up gravel and dirt. Aimed right for her house.

Blinded by the oversize headlights on the Silverado 3500, Trey shifted, then dived to the side, before he became part of the colossal push bumper. He scooted to his feet and turned as the truck skidded to a stop, inches from colliding with his patrol pickup. This guy was out of control.

He glanced over his shoulder.

Justine stood on the porch, watching.

"Get in the house." Unable to view inside the cab, Trey approached with caution. "Driver, put your hands where I can see them."

"I want out of this death trap!" a man bellowed. The passenger door flung wide, and a cowboy boot emerged.

"Slowly," Trey demanded.

The sixtysomething man disembarked awkwardly, straightened his black Stetson, then tossed out a backpack. "Arrest him! That boy tried to kill me!"

"Driver, shut off the engine and climb down with your hands visible to me at all times." Trey stood at a distance, maintaining visual on the driver and passenger.

"His name is Nathan Yancy. Just got his license, and his dad assured me he was capable. I saw my life flash before my eyes ten times in five miles!"

A nervous-looking teenager held up shaking hands, his body turned sideways to exit. "Sorry, sir. I'm not used to my dad's pickup." His voice quivered over the engine's rumble.

"Don't go blaming the truck, boy!" The passenger stormed toward Trey. "I'm Will Percy. I work for

Justine." He started for the porch, halted by Magnum's growls. "You got another dog? What's wrong with this one?"

"Nathan, turn off the engine and join me." Trey kept one eye on Will. "Mr. Percy, that's K-9 Magnum. Stay where you are and keep your hands visible at all times."

"I ain't no criminal!"

"Will's my employee. Do what Trooper Jackson says," Justine stated.

The willowy teenager killed the diesel and in almost slow motion jumped down, landing steadily on his cowboy boots, arms in the air, looking more of a gymnast than frenzied novice. He shifted from one foot to another.

Trey holstered his gun. "Relax and lower your arms. I need to see your driver's license."

The boy produced the identification with a shaky hand. "I gave Mr. Percy a ride—"

"You tried to kill me!"

Trey took the card and silenced Will with a look. "Hmm, got it today?"

"Yes, sir." Nathan swallowed, bobbing his Adam's apple, and nibbled on a nonexistent fingernail.

"Congratulations." Trey handed back the card and lowered his voice. "The day I got my license, I sank my dad's new truck, trying to impress a bunch of girls at the lake. Thought I could load the boat on the trailer by myself. Accidentally left the truck in Reverse. Went down faster than the *Titanic*."

Nathan gasped. "Wow." The boy's cheeks flushed a bright red and his eyes were wide as dinner plates. "My dad woulda grounded me forever. Same as he's gonna do when Mr. Percy tells him about tonight."

"You'll be fine. Just take it easy. You're free to go."

"Thank you." Nathan nodded so vigorously Trey thought the kid's head might bounce off his neck.

"He's gonna kill someone!" Will used his Stetson to gesture at the pickup.

"Sir, you must calm down." Trey focused on Magnum and spoke the cease command. *"Nein."*

Will clamped his mouth shut, fury in his expression.

"Will's harmless," Justine whispered.

Maybe so, but Trey never second-guessed Magnum's instincts.

"I didn't think you'd be here until morning," Justine said.

"Finished at Yancy's early." Will's eyes stayed on Magnum.

Justine smiled. "Great. I'll get on the road sooner."

The roar of the diesel's engine captured their attention as Nathan performed an excruciating forty-point turn near the garage. After several near misses—including the barn, fence and a tree—the dually rumbled at a snail's pace from the property.

"Yancy better pay up his auto insurance," Will grumbled, appraising Trey with obvious disdain. "Who're you?"

Trey bristled and bit back a smart answer, extending a hand. "Trooper Trey Jackson. Is Will short for William?"

"Wilbur."

"Trey and I know each other from a long time ago," Justine replied. "He's here on a professional visit."

"In the dead of night?" He harrumphed. "I'm heading to bed."

"Okay. List is on the fridge."

Will grunted, hefting his backpack. With a final adjustment to his Stetson, he walked to the barn.

The guy bugged Trey, giving rise to a hundred probing questions. He started with the most significant. "He doesn't stay in the house?" The farther the proximity to Justine, the better.

"No. His accommodations are in the barn."

"What's Will do?"

Justine lowered her voice and waved Trey around the porch to the front door. "He works part-time for me and other ranches in the area wherever the labor takes him. I'd hire him full-time, but that's not possible right now."

Was Will involved in Justine's kidnapping? "How long have you known him?"

"About nine months." She raised a hand and brow. "Don't go there. He cares for the boys when I go out of town."

"Seems like a real animal lover." Trey didn't try to hide the sarcasm in his voice.

"That's a defense mechanism. He's a softy and a hard worker."

"Let's talk in private. After I take your full report, I'll explain why I was coming to see you this evening."

She hesitated by the door. "Can I borrow your flashlight? I think the kidnapper messed with my fuse box to lure me into the basement."

"I'll reset it. Point me in the direction. I'd like to clear the house."

She folded her arms, but her tone held relief. "Basement door is in the hall on the right."

"Magnum, stay."

The dog whined but obeyed. Poor guy loved building clearance, but with the stairs in the multistoried farmhouse, Trey couldn't risk a reinjury.

He started with the upper level, making his way to the basement, avoiding the personal items and an abundance of file boxes spread across the floor.

Finally, he located the antiquated fuse box and the fuse the subject must've removed. He inserted the fuse, illuminating the musty space. Trey collected a butcher knife and broken flashlight from the ground and returned to the kitchen, where Justine stood, Magnum dutifully keeping watch.

The lights made the destruction worse than he'd first glimpsed, and by her pained expression, it was a shock to Justine. "He was busy while I was in the trunk."

"What was he searching for?" Trey placed the knife and flashlight on the counter.

"Hard to say."

Except her mannerism said otherwise.

She led him to the sofa and perched on the far edge. "It's late. What do you need to file the report?"

He sat and Magnum lay at his feet with a sigh. Trey withdrew his notebook. "What happened right before you walked down to the basement?"

"I was reading, and the lights flickered, then went out." She hesitated, hand on her khaki shorts pocket, drawing attention to the small book-sized bulge he'd noticed before. "Wait. Why were you coming to see me?"

Pops said relationships were like bank accounts. You had to deposit trust before you withdrew. "Kayla Nolan's cold case."

"You're not the investigator." Her accusatory tone bit, and he absorbed the blow. She winced. "I didn't realize you worked cold cases."

Trey glanced at Magnum. "We're on a hiatus until his paw heals. Besides, the original investigator retired a long time ago."

"Isn't there a conflict of interest?"

Why the third degree? A chance to fling guilt knives for his failure to protect Kayla? Trey shoved away his defensiveness. He'd own his failures. "Sergeant Oliver assigned me and sends his apologies for Callista's behavior."

Justine's posture softened. "She wasn't very nice."

"Don't take it personally. She was in a hurry to get out of the office on a Friday afternoon. Anyway, what made you call in?"

Justine bit her lip.

Trey's impatience won out. "We'll get a lot further if we put down the shields."

She pulled a brown leather journal from her pocket and held it up but out of his reach. "I found Kayla's diary this afternoon, moving stuff from the Dog House. No clue how it's gone unnoticed all these years or why it was in my things. Although, Kayla stayed at my place a lot before…" Her voice trailed off. "Anyway, she must've left it by accident. Based on some of her entries, I'll develop a profile to help identify the killer or narrow down possible suspects. I'm certain they were acquaintances."

"Her case is identified as a suspicious death, not murder."

"Semantics. And no matter what they said, Kayla didn't use drugs."

Was Justine in denial about her friend's addiction? She knew Kayla better than he, though Trey didn't recall witnessing Kayla in an inebriated state during their social gatherings. "Who else knows about the diary?"

"I told Kayla's parents when I contacted them about reopening the file and asked to meet with them."

Wealthy and prominent in the Lincoln community, the Nolans weren't exactly down-to-earth folks, from what he'd heard. "Did they agree to speak to you?"

"After some persuasion." Justine fidgeted with a thread on the couch. "I'm sure my call came as a shock."

"I'll take that as a no."

"I'm not quick to judge. Like some people." She narrowed her eyes. "Trauma affects people in unique ways. Dredging up old memories is painful."

Trey noted the Nolans on his list of possible suspects.

Magnum's ears perked up, and he got to his feet, sniffing the air by the open window. He roved in deliberate precision around the room before pausing by the door.

"Hey, Mags, what's up?"

"Probably needs out," Justine said.

Trey didn't agree. Magnum's actions indicated unease, but he didn't want to scare her. "I'll be right back."

Trey glanced out the side window before opening the door.

Fireflies flickered in the distance, and the porch light illuminated a small area. Had the kidnapper been stupid and returned?

Stranger things had happened. "Lock the door behind me. If I'm not back in ten minutes, call 9-1-1."

THREE

Trey set Magnum on the grassy area beside the porch steps. "Have at it."

Magnum took off at a modified pace in full-search mode. Perhaps he should've leashed the dog, but giving him free rein on the property seemed to energize him.

The Belgian Malinois ducked into the tree line on the north side of the expansive ranch.

"Magnum!"

Traversing the uneven ground in the dark was challenging, but Magnum appeared undeterred and determined. He actively sniffed his way into a thicket of overgrown weeds, bushes and dead branches.

Trey activated his weapon's attached flashlight and swept the beam across the darkened area. He spotted Magnum's tail as he disappeared into the thick brambles where ticks and other things Trey preferred to avoid lived in abundance. "Ah, dude, do you have to go in there?"

He groaned and caught up with Magnum, slowing at the forest opening. Long branches heavy with green summer leaves hovered like arms. Bushes reached up in a wild stretch of thick briars restricting his entrance. A breeze rustled the foliage and something buzzed past Trey's ear. He swatted it away.

"Magnum." Worry niggled through him. Trey called louder, "Magnum."

Sweeping the light across the thicket, he spotted Magnum sniffing the earth beneath a large oak tree. He circled the wide trunk, disappearing behind the massive circumference of bark. Trey hurried to the space, stomping over the knobby roots and rock-covered ground. He dodged a tangle of low-hanging twigs and gripped a branch before it clotheslined him.

His fingers brushed something thin, and Trey jerked back his hand.

Snake?

Magnum barked, startling Trey and regaining his attention. He shifted the light to the dog. A length of rope dangled from above. Trey traced the braid higher to the leftovers of a makeshift tree house situated between the branches.

Magnum scurried to the opposite side of the trunk, and Trey followed him around the base of the tree to get a better look. Spotting nothing of concern, he leaned down and snapped on Magnum's leash. "No more of that, mister. We don't need any further injuries. Sorry, but you're going to have to stay with me."

A plank of wood tumbled from the tree house. Trey ducked and turned just as an explosion of pain to the back of his head sent him stumbling forward.

A dull thud and fluttering on the opposite side of the tree had Trey swinging the light downward.

Magnum rushed to investigate, and Trey caught a glimpse of something nestled in the tall grass. A soft whizzing emitted.

Magnum tilted his head and swayed slightly.

A snap above drew Trey's attention. A second plank toppled, striking Trey's face and exploding pain. He dropped the leash, covering his bleeding nose with his hands.

The plank landed beside him. Trey stepped forward, caught by a tightening around his throat that yanked him back. His fingers groped, desperate to stop the rope from strangling him.

The force dragged Trey against the tree, then pulled him upward.

He kicked, girded his weight and dug his boots into the trunk for leverage. The deathly battle had Trey doing a strange backward climb up the tree to keep from being strangled while groping for his weapon. The criminal pulled higher, cutting off Trey's air flow. Panicking, he wrapped his hand around the rope with one hand and grappled for his gun with the other.

At last, he tugged the weapon free from his holster.

The perp jerked harder, and Trey lost his grip on the gun. It plunged to the ground, out of reach.

The need to breathe outweighed everything else.

Stars danced before his eyes.

Trey fought to stay conscious as the perp hefted him higher.

Forced to stand on his tiptoes, Trey gasped for air.

He was fading. His body flattened against the trunk.

Where was Magnum? Why wasn't he barking?

Trey tried to look up, but the hold was too tight. He could barely move. His head brushed against the rough bark, scraping his scalp.

His eyes bulged from their sockets.

Desperate for air.

Desperate to stay conscious. He continued stretching his arms upward, grasping at the rope. It grew tauter.

Justine. He had to stay awake for Justine.

Lord. Help!

Trey's lungs burned. Gravity tugged his arms and legs down.

The darkness swooped in, consuming him.

Dragging him into the abyss.

Consumed by the shadows, Trey closed his eyes and surrendered.

"Hey! Wake up!" A voice hovered from somewhere far away.

Magnum's familiar bark.

A slap and a sting on his face jolted Trey conscious.

"Trooper! Wake up!"

A second slap caused his eyes to fly open. Trey blinked against the blinding light, shielding his face from the brightness.

With a groan, Trey shifted, pushing himself up

from the hard ground, and took in his surroundings. Magnum barked furiously from beneath a nearby tree. His leash was wrapped around a low-hanging branch.

The light altered, and Will moved in front of him, staring down. "'Bout time you come to," he grumbled, offering a hand to help Trey stand.

After steadying himself, still woozy, Trey rushed to free Magnum and stumbled over an exposed tree root. "What happened?"

His head swam and a dull headache pulsed at the base of his neck. He leaned down, checking Magnum for any injuries, grateful to find none. But that didn't explain how his dog had ended up bound so far away from him.

Trey recalled the whizzing sound before Magnum went silent. Had the perp drugged his dog?

He untied the leash, and Magnum shifted protectively in front of him, creating a barrier between him and Will.

Had Will attacked him from the tree house?

Magnum didn't rush at Will, but his hackles were raised.

Trey needed information, and at the moment, Will was the only one capable of providing that benefit. "Why was my dog tied up over there?"

Magnum emitted a low growl.

"You gonna call him off or not?" Will groused.

Keeping a wary eye on Will, Trey reached for his gun, then remembered he'd dropped it.

"Whatcha looking for?"

"My gun," Trey confessed.

Will shifted the flashlight, illuminating the area, and Trey scanned the ground for his weapon.

Magnum's disposition grew edgier. "My dog sure seems to have a problem with you. Any idea why that is?"

Will seemed oblivious to Trey's concerns, his blank expression as hard to read as invisible ink. "I don't speak dumb mutt."

Trey's gaze moved to a pistol resting in Will's waistband. Was Will a friend or foe?

"You're welcome," Will grumbled. "Look here, Trooper, I just saved your life. Least you can do is call off your dog."

"You know the funny thing about animals? They tend to pick up on cues and nuances humans miss."

"That so? They also chase squirrels and bark at leaves." Will crossed his arms. "And your dog didn't wake you either."

Trey chuckled despite his hesitation. "Can't argue that. Magnum, *nein*."

Magnum dropped to a sit beside Trey. "Thank you for helping me."

If Trey had to guess based on their short inter-actions and his cop instincts, Will was the kind of guy who enjoyed riling a person, then when he got punched, claimed he was attacked unprovoked. At least he was consistent in his rudeness. *Kill 'em with kindness*, Pops would say. And right now, Trey needed details. "I'm at a loss, so anything you can tell me would be helpful. Starting with, how'd my dog end up over there?"

"Couldn't tell ya. He was rabid, and I wasn't going anywhere near him."

Magnum was far from *rabid*, but Trey didn't correct Will since he was volunteering information. "How did you know I was out here?"

"I didn't. Your dog barked up a storm and woke me out of a dead sleep. Came out here to give you a piece of my mind and found you sprawled cold under the tree. I figured the mutt wouldn't let me near enough to release the leash, so I left him tied up over there, then helped you."

Trey returned to Will, standing where the assault had occurred. Two planks of wood lay on the ground. His gaze traveled up the trunk to the tree house. "There was someone hiding there. He ambushed me."

"So, that's where you got the bloody nose."

Trey glanced down. The dark uniform hid the crimson stains, but his nose ached with confirmation. "Yeah, whacked me with a plank, then tried strangling me."

Will pointed the flashlight into the tree. A rope swung, tethered by a pulley near the remnants of the tree house. "Why would someone go to all that effort?"

Trey jerked to face the farmhouse. "Is Justine okay?"

"Why wouldn't she be? Ain't seen nobody around here, and other than your dog's rowdy caterwauling, it's been quiet. I sat here trying to wake your sorry self up for the past fifteen minutes."

Had Justine told Will about the kidnapping? Trey scoured his mind, recalling the interaction. No. She'd never mentioned it. If Will was involved, was he playing dumb? Or did he not realize Justine was in danger? Anxious to get to her, Trey headed out of the brambles. "How long was I out?"

"Couldn't tell you." Will joined him.

"I need to check on Justine."

"Seems to me you should be more concerned with whoever attacked you." Will grunted, shifting the light to illuminate a path.

"Unless they did it to get me out of the way." Trey shot Will a quizzical glance.

"Of what?"

Trey kept walking, unwilling to give him any unnecessary information, still unsure of the man. Magnum remained close to his side, and they cut across the pasture.

"Why are you here, Trooper?" Will persisted.

Trey didn't look at him, his focus fixed on the farmhouse. No lights shone from inside. *Please let Justine be safely asleep.* But Trey's instincts warned that wasn't true. "Justine and I are working on a case. I've known her a long time."

"Funny, she's never mentioned you."

Trey winced. Not speaking of him was better than

telling the whole world how much she detested him. He hadn't spotted a Trey-shaped dartboard. That was a positive, and although she hadn't been oozing with kindness, she'd been decent in their communications.

"I haven't seen her for a while."

"This yours?" Will called.

Trey halted and turned, then walked to where Will stood beside his gun.

"Yes." Snagging the weapon, Trey checked the bullets. All removed. Convenient. And how did Will just happen to know where to find it? Trey tucked the Glock into his holster. Why remove his gun and then leave it lying on the ground? He continued the trek across the pasture. "Did you see anyone?"

"Nope. In case you ain't noticed, Trooper, light isn't really plentiful out here."

"Did you hear anything? A vehicle?"

Will snorted. "You got dirt in your ears? Your dog was it."

Trey increased his pace, desperate to get to Justine. They reached the edge of the yard just as an ear-piercing blast exploded.

The force had Trey ducking and protecting Magnum.

Trey turned, shielding his eyes from the consuming flash of light engulfing the house. Ears ringing with agonizing intensity, Trey pressed a hand against his head to still the noise. He blinked to clear his vision. "Justine!"

Jumping to his feet, he bolted for the home, Magnum running beside him in an awkward three-legged gait. Why were his limbs so heavy? Trey pumped his arms, willing his body to get to Justine faster.

Please, God, let her be alive.

His mind raced. Less than an hour since finding Justine, and he'd lost her.

Why had he left her alone? He'd stood not more than twenty feet away, wasting precious time with Will while some maniac hurt Justine.

Trey had failed to protect someone.

Again.

She would die tonight. Justine squeezed her eyes against the blinding explosion of light emitting from her farmhouse and prayed the home didn't go up in flames.

Lord, not fire. Please not ever again.

Even from her position beneath the canopy of trees at the far side of the ranch, her ears rang from the blast.

She recognized the diversion tactic, a sort of flash-bang, typically used by law enforcement. Though how her captor had managed to set it off from a remote detonation device eluded her.

"That'll keep 'em busy." Her captor chuckled.

"Don't hurt them!"

He snorted. "Shut up. You better be grateful I didn't kill the cop and his mutt." Under his breath, he mumbled, "Shoulda double dosed the dog though. We coulda been long gone by now if he hadn't barked and woke the old codger."

He'd drugged Magnum? That explained why he hadn't alerted Trey.

The man glared at her. "Woulda saved us both some trouble if you'd just handed over the book. I came prepared this time."

Justine jerked to look at him, his comment confirming he was the same man who'd abducted her earlier in the evening. She watched in horror as Trey, Magnum and Will bounded from the far pasture. Grateful they were alive, she stared helplessly as they called out her name.

They'd search the house, and by the time they realized she wasn't there, she'd be dead. The overgrown foliage that bordered the north side of her property provided the camouflage her captor needed and prevented the men from seeing her.

Had the whole scene not been terrifying, she'd assess the criminal's distraction as rather ingenious. Though she wasn't gagged, the sharp tip of the gun's muzzle pressed against the back of her head kept her quiet and at his mercy. What recourse did she have but to obey him and pray she found a way of escape? Or if she gave him the diary, maybe he'd let her go.

No superhero to rescue her.

She was on her own.

The man made no effort to disguise himself. An indicator he intended to kill her.

Dead people couldn't testify.

"There's nothing in the diary. Why do you want it?" she blurted, working her negotiator-skills training for all it was worth.

"Too late. You had your chance to hand over the book. Now you can deal with them."

"Them?" Who did he work for? *Keep him talking.*

"Justine!" Trey's cries carried across the land, tearing at her heart.

"Hel—" Her plea was cut off by her captor's boa constrictor arm encircling her neck. The gun pressed harder against her temple.

The man dragged her deeper into the tree line. His hold squeezed the air from her lungs. She kicked, fighting to breathe.

He loosened his grip and shoved a gag in her mouth, then secured it with a piece of tape. He finished the adornment with zip ties around her wrists. Her one advantage was he didn't bind her arms behind her. But timing was crucial.

"Don't get no bright ideas. Try to run and I'll break your legs."

Somehow, she didn't doubt his threat, and since he hadn't bound her ankles again, she'd take the win.

"You can be a good girl and shimmy between the wires. Or I'll just throw you over."

Justine swallowed against the gag that eliminated any chance of speaking. She nodded.

"Smart." He went first, ducking between the fence cables. His beefy hand gripped her arm, yanking Justine forward.

She maneuvered through, catching her shoe on the wire and stumbling. She reached out to stop her fall, but the man's grip tightened, and he tugged harder, sending a volt of agony up her arm. He jerked again, nearly pulling Justine's shoulder out of the socket.

The gag muffled her cry of pain.

He lugged her to a four-seater UTV parked and hidden behind a large bale of hay. Justine recognized Richardson's three hundred acres. A cow mooed nearby, as if confirming her supposition.

Would Richardson hear her if she screamed?

"Don't even think about it," the perp warned, as though hearing her thoughts. "Make one sound, and they're all dead. Including your mutts."

Justine's mind whirled with possibilities and none of them pleasant. She had to escape before they got in the UTV.

"Get in."

An idea bloomed. He was at least a foot taller than her. She'd need to stand on the floorboards to be eye level with him.

Justine clamped her hands together, forming a large fist, while he assisted her onto the UTV. She turned and thrust her bound wrists upward.

The crack of his nose confirmed solid contact.

He swore. Then, in a flash, he retaliated by smacking her with a powerful slap across the face.

Justine flew backward, landing hard on the ground beside the UTV. She scrambled to her feet, and using the vehicle as a barrier, she scurried around it.

"I'm going to kill you!" The man stalked her, arms outstretched like a wide net. He dodged from side to side, cackling as he toyed with her.

Justine surveyed the distance. For all his bulk, she prayed he wasn't fast.

She jumped to the right, faking him out, then lunged in the opposite direction, straining for the freedom beyond the fence line. Her bound wrists made running difficult, but Justine pushed on.

Heavy pounding and breaths behind her propelled Justine to run harder.

Almost there.

The diary beat against her thigh, hidden inside her khaki shorts pocket.

Justine's fingers grazed the fence just as the man tackled her to the ground, knocking the wind from her lungs. His hands were on her ankles in an instant. He yanked her back, flipping her over.

"You'll pay for that." He hefted Justine into the air and hoisted her over his shoulder.

The impact and constant jolting of her stomach sent a wave of nausea through her. She swallowed down the rising bile burning her throat. With her bound arms, she stretched out her fingers, grasping the corner of the tape, and tugged. The tape ripped the gag out too, and she dropped both.

Justine tried to scream, but the lack of breath diluted the sound.

The man's massive torso was like a brick wall, yet she was unrelenting. Justine fought and kicked against his stranglehold on her legs. He squeezed tighter, and shooting pain exploded through her thighs.

She refused to give in.

With her bound hands, she beat on his back, aiming for his kidneys. Twice she made contact, and the man jerked in spasm. On her third attempt, she struck pay dirt.

He lost his hold, dropping Justine. She landed on the hard ground next to the UTV. Air whooshed from her lungs, and she gasped.

Before she could respond, the man's Texas-sized boot settled on her chest, pinning her in place.

He reached up and grabbed something from the front seat. Then he squatted beside her, smothering her face with a cloth.

Her nose filled with a sickening sweet smell.

Ether.

Justine held her breath, willing her body not to inhale the anesthetic. She had only seconds before she'd be forced to breathe.

She wriggled, turning her head from side to side. He was linebacker huge and unyielding.

The battle to stay conscious warred with her body's desperation for oxygen. Justine's vision blurred, and her eyes bulged from the pressure. Her lungs were ablaze, exploding behind her rib cage.

Not yet.

Her attacker knelt on her chest, pressing the cloth harder over her face.

If she didn't get free, she'd pass out for real.

Air. She needed air.

And fast.

Lord, I can't hold on anymore. Please help me.

Fake him out. The thought sprouted to her mind unbidden, providing the only option left. Convince him she'd gone unconscious. Justine stopped fighting and closed her eyes, allowing her other senses to heighten.

The boot weight lifted from her chest, and he hoisted her up in a fireman's carry.

The cloth fell to the ground, and Justine inhaled slowly so as not to draw attention, though her lungs begged for more. He laid her across what she assumed was the back seat of the UTV. Then the vehicle rocked as he slid behind the steering wheel.

Justine opened her eyes.

The engine roared to life.

This was her one chance.

When the UTV lurched forward, Justine rolled off the seat, onto the floorboard, and pushed up to her knees. She leaped off the side and into the pasture.

With hands still bound, she sprinted for the fence.

"Trey! Will! Help!"

The UTV turned, headlights beaming behind her. He was coming back!

Justine swerved, rounding a hay bale, and lunged for the fence line.

She reached the wires and ducked between them. "Trey! Will!"

Light bounced from the porch, a beacon calling her home.

Justine ran with everything in her. "Help!"

Barks erupted, and she aimed for the familiar sight of the Belgian Malinois hobbling across the property.

The UTV stopped, changed direction, and the whir of the engine faded behind her.

Justine didn't look back.

"Justine!" Trey closed the distance between them, but Magnum reached her first.

She fell to her knees, chest heaving with exertion, and fought to catch her breath.

Trey braced and helped Justine to stand. "What happened?"

"He. I. Eth." Justine couldn't get out the words.

"It's okay. Just breathe," Trey said, holding on to her.

She crumpled against him. Needing his strength.

Will hurried up beside them. "What happened?" The grumpy exterior was gone, and he reached for her. "Are you okay?"

Dizziness consumed Justine, and she swayed.

Finally catching her breath, she said, "The same man from earlier. He got away. On the UTV. Richardson's land."

"And he used the flash-bang to distract us," Trey assessed.

Justine nodded.

"Let's get you inside."

The group made their way across the property and into the house. The smell of smoke filled the living room, increasing Justine's nausea. Childhood memories flooded her mind, creating a vise over her chest.

"I need air." She rushed to the swing and inhaled long and deep, clearing her lungs. Justine gripped the banister, anchoring her shaking body to the porch.

Trey joined her. "We have to leave."

Justine shook her head. "No. Not until I'm sure the boys are safe."

"They're fine, and I'll be here to watch over them," Will assured her.

"See?" Trey pleaded. "Justine, we need to get out of here. We'll work on a sketch of the guy while your memory is fresh. There's a great artist in Lincoln."

Justine dropped onto the porch swing, gazing out on the inky landscape. Anger ignited. "I can draw the sketch myself. This is my home. No bully is scaring me off my land."

Trey sighed. "Will, would you mind giving us a minute alone?"

She glanced up. Her hired hand hesitated, gaze bouncing between Justine and Trey.

"If the guy returns, we need to make sure we're ready. Do you have any other weapons?" Trey asked.

Will nodded. "Yeah. Ain't no one getting close to Justine again." He stepped off the porch. "I'll check the garage and my stash."

After he'd disappeared around the side of the house, Justine said, "Trey, I can't leave the boys. If anything happened to them…"

"Will promised to take care of your dogs. If I have to ask my brother to come and haul the whole crew to my home, I'll do it."

She laughed at the image.

"I'll request Slade patrol the property personally. Whatever it takes. Okay?" Trey's blue eyes bored into her, embracing her. How long since someone had offered to reach out a helping hand?

No. Dependency was a trap that morphed into a weakness.

Justine averted her gaze and changed the topic. "Slade's still a trooper?" Fabulous.

She'd known Trey's older brother, Slade, only as an acquaintance when they'd attended the same social events. But the family was renowned. The kind of people who'd warn Trey away from less than desirables.

Like me.

"He'd love to see you."

A happy reunion invading her ranch solace, where she'd just escaped with her life, wasn't in her plans. "I've unleashed a monster. Who wants the diary so bad? I haven't seen anything so incriminating it'll pinpoint one specific person. At least, not yet."

"Clearly someone fears the contents."

Justine filled Trey in on the encounter.

"He drugged my dog? That explains a lot." Trey leaned against the spindled porch rails. "How did you get over there?"

"I should've listened to you. I heard meowing from the far side of the house. I always leave the windows open. You've experienced firsthand how stuffy the place gets. Anyway, I was looking for Clover. Thought she locked herself in the closet again. She does that sometimes. When I reached the back room, the sound came from near the window. I leaned out to call to her." She swallowed, shivering at the memory. "He dragged me through before I realized what was happening."

Trey ran a hand over his head. "I never should've left you. I didn't think the guy would have the nerve to show up again tonight."

"Did he hurt you or Magnum?" Her mind reeled at Trey's breakdown of the night's events. "Thankfully, he didn't kill all of you and Will found you when he did."

Trey hesitated a moment too long.

"What are you trying not to say?"

"Have you considered the possibility Will's working with this maniac?"

She opened her mouth to argue, but Trey held up his hand. "Hear me out."

Justine bit her lip.

"I'll be honest—I'm not sure what to think of Will. He could've killed me and didn't. But he might've lured me outside to give the kidnapper time to get to you."

"No, Will helped you," Justine insisted.

"Consider this. The distance from the thicket to the house is expansive. He couldn't be in two places at once. If Will was the one hiding in the tree, he would've been perfectly placed to knock me unconscious."

She couldn't refute the argument beyond a shadow of a doubt. At least, not to Trey's satisfaction. But in her heart, she knew Will wouldn't do that.

Still, she'd been a bad judge of character once before... Thoughts of her ex-fiancé Simon returned. He'd blinded her with false promises for their life together while stealing everything she owned. Thanks to Simon's betrayal, Justine learned the importance of caution and careful behavioral assessments.

Justine shook her head, then stopped when the world started spinning. "No way. Will isn't like you think. You've misjudged him. You saw how upset he was."

Trey shrugged. "You have to admit the events were conveniently timed."

Justine averted her eyes. No. Admitting Will was a criminal meant she'd inaccurately assessed her employee. Behavioral science was her forte. Her superpower. The one thing besides her animals that gave her life meaning.

Misjudging Will meant she'd failed to identify a traitor under her roof. And if she couldn't spot an offender under her own nose, how could she correctly perform her job in other cases? Most important, how could she develop the profile for Kayla's case?

Failure meant she was incapable of her profession.

Failure wasn't an option.

"I understand you not wanting to leave your home, but I think it's evident whoever is after this diary isn't going to stop."

"I agree, but it's late. Surely the guy won't return tonight."

Trey withdrew his notepad. "Let's run through everything you remember. Did the kidnapper say anything?"

Justine sighed. "He demanded to know where 'it' was. Though he never mentioned the diary, I assume that's what he referred to. He also said I'd have to deal with them. Whoever 'them' is."

"That adds credence to a hired thug."

"I did think it was strange he used my car to kidnap me the first time, and we never saw anyone approach the second. Either he parked nearby and walked the rest of the way or someone dropped him off."

"Will doesn't own a vehicle."

Justine glared, disapproval hanging between them. "Will knows the topography of the area."

"You lost me."

"The kidnapper didn't slow for the big pothole on the road."

"Why is that important?"

"His lack of knowledge indicates he isn't a local. After the heavy flooding from the recent rains, many of the dirt roads were washed away or damaged. Will's familiar with the landscape."

"Hmm. Interesting."

"What's it going to take for you to believe Will is innocent? He'd never hurt me. But I'd appreciate extra patrolling by Slade or whoever if you'd arrange it."

Trey sighed. "Justine—"

"This is my life and my home. I'm perfectly capable of making the necessary decisions." And if she was wrong, she would die at the hands of Kayla's killer.

FOUR

A wet swipe across his face and a warm puff of air dragged Trey to consciousness. He stared at the familiar brown eyes pleading with him. "Mags, I'm a light sleeper. A simple whine works to wake me."

Trey sat up on the living room sofa with a grunt, ruffling the Malinois's mane. His gaze traveled past the padded dog bed Justine had provided for Magnum and landed on the hands of the antique grandfather clock. 5:45 a.m.

He stood and stretched, feeling the repercussions of sleeping on the couch after declining Justine's offer of her spare bedroom. Proximity to the main floor overrode his personal comfort.

A text from Slade buzzed from his cell phone. ETA five.

His brother's overnight security detail had allowed Trey a short but needed rest, and the night had passed uneventfully. Otherwise, he'd be functioning on no sleep, which was worse than a backache.

Magnum whined and thumped his tail in a steady get-moving-please-now rhythm.

"I'm coming." Trey schlepped to the window and peered out before tugging open the door.

Magnum wasted no time scurrying outside.

"Wait."

But the dog was halfway across the lawn, after

an almost normal descent down the stairs. He didn't favor his good side as much. A definite sign of healing. "Guess you're feeling better."

A cardinal trilled from one of the maple trees, and Trey filled his lungs with the fresh morning air. He strolled the wraparound porch, maintaining visual of Magnum actively exploring the ranch.

Pastel streaks colored the sky as the sun peeked over the horizon. Ominous land the night before, it now splayed out in a lush green landscape.

"I could get used to this," Trey mumbled to no one, stepping off the porch.

Magnum joined him, nose to the ground.

Slade's familiar blue sedan pulled into the driveway and parked near Trey's patrol vehicle.

"Good morning, sunshine. Packed for a trip?" Slade stepped out of his car.

Trey blinked. "Dude, I just woke up and I'm caffeine deficient. What're you talking about?"

"Those bags under your eyes. If they get any bigger, your head will fall in," Slade teased.

Trey ran a hand over the stubble on his face. "Thanks, bro."

"Brought what you asked for." Slade passed Trey a small bag, which he transferred to his patrol truck's tailgate cabinets. He returned to find Slade offering a supersize fountain drink. "Mountain Dew?"

Trey wrinkled his nose. "Um. No."

"Suit yourself." Slade took a long swig. "This

place is nice, but I can see why you needed the perimeter help. Did you get any sleep?"

Trey leaned against Slade's car. "Yeah, a few hours. If you hadn't shown up, I'd be a zombie."

"Good thing you caught me when you did. Although, you might owe Asia some cinnamon rolls for interrupting my off days."

Trey chuckled at the mention of Slade's wife. "I'll make it up to her. However, you're probably donating this time."

Slade shrugged. "It's all good. I've got your six." His brother referred to the cop slang for defending and covering one another. "Family first. Always. You really should relocate her for now."

"I tried. Even explained the need for a sketch artist while the image of the criminal's ugly mug was fresh in Justine's mind. She refused and said she'd do it herself." Trey paced a short space in front of Slade. "I get it though. She's concerned for her foster dogs."

"You two are a perfect match. Both dog motivated and stubborn."

Warmth radiated up Trey's neck at the implication of being matched with Justine. Ridiculous and out of the question. He was the last person she'd consider dating since she blamed him for Kayla's death. Justine believed Trey had failed to show up when Kayla called. If he'd been there, maybe he could've stopped her from overdosing. Yet he hadn't even known Kayla had a drug abuse problem? No.

He wasn't relationship material. Last night's double failure in apprehending the kidnapper proved Trey's inability to protect those he cared about. Romance wasn't an option for either of them.

Oblivious to Trey's internal debate, Slade continued, "If Justine refuses to leave, Oliver might finagle overtime for security detail."

"Doubtful. He made a point last night of reminding me how short-staffed we are."

"Yeah, little brother, you're still taking after me, even with trouble and impossible odds perched on your shoulders."

Trey bristled slightly at the reminder—always shadowed by his older sibling. It was no secret Trey had looked up to Slade when they were younger, but they weren't kids anymore. Was calling him for help a mistake? Yet what choice did he have?

"Don't get your feathers all ruffled. I'm only teasing." Slade took another swig of soda. "What's Oliver got you working?"

And there it was, the piece Trey hadn't shared. Once he mentioned Kayla's name, Slade's older-sibling, unwanted advice would spill out.

Trey inhaled. "Kayla Nolan's case."

"Murder."

"Technically, no. It's labeled a drug buy gone bad resulting in a suspicious overdose death. Kayla was attacked in her apartment. Murder isn't out of the question. Justine's developing a profile of the killer." Before Slade could interrupt, Trey launched into an explanation regarding the diary and their planned visit with the Nolans later in the day.

A beat passed. "Just curious, but what does she hope to gain by meeting with them?"

"Something about a clinical perspective versus conclusions based off memories from things Kayla had shared."

"I guess that makes sense. Memories have a way of tainting everything."

And they dredged up pain you'd forgotten existed. Trey shoved away the thought. "Should've seen the look on her face when I asked what time 'we' were heading out."

"She didn't want you along for the ride, I'm guessing? How'd you convince her?"

"With my brilliant power of persuasion." Trey chuckled.

"No, really." Slade quirked a brow.

"Well, there is the fact that the files belong to the patrol, and I can't just hand those over and leave."

"'Possession is nine-tenths of the law,'" Slade quoted teasingly, then lowered his voice. "Dude, are you sure being involved in this case is a good idea?"

There it was. Big-brother judgment. "What choice do I have? I owe Kayla."

Slade shook his head. "Trey, her death wasn't your fault. You didn't have any other options. Let it go."

Heaviness weighted his chest. "Too late. I'm committed to getting justice for Kayla. Justine's profile and the diary might provide the missing leads, after all these years."

"Do what you need to. Just let me know if you want me out here again tonight."

"Thanks. Hey, one more favor?"

"Sure."

"Run a background for me?"

Slade surveyed the grounds. "On who?"

"Justine's hired hand, Wilbur Percy."

"Stetson Man? He trolled the property until late last night. Is he a problem?"

"I'm not sure. I need evidence to either kill my suspicions or convince Justine he's not the man she thinks he is," Trey said.

A creaking drew the men's attention.

Slade gave a jerk of his chin. "Speaking of."

Four of the five canines lumbered out of the barn, scattering in all directions. The basset hound Justine called Barney followed Will outside. He knelt, stroking the dog's head, and spoke too softly for Trey to hear. For all his complaining about the animals, he appeared gentle and kind with them.

Contemplating Magnum's earlier assessment, Trey wasn't sure what to make of Will. Still, if his partner found fault with the man, Trey would remain wary. Though this morning Magnum strolled toward the other dogs, undaunted by Will's presence.

As if Will heard Trey's thoughts, he turned and visibly stiffened. Will gave a slight tip of his Stetson before shoving his hands into his jean pockets. Trey didn't miss the pistol tucked into Will's waistband. At least he took his role seriously. Trey waved him over, and Will's reluctance registered in his every step, closing the distance.

"Will, this is my brother, Slade," Trey said.

Slade extended a hand.

"Nice to meet you. Saw you driving around last evening." Will's reply sounded more like a complaint than a greeting.

"Thankfully, it was a quiet night. I'll head out. Touch base with me later, Trey." Slade slid behind the wheel of his car and started the engine.

Will moved toward a midsize brown dog sniffing near a large trash receptacle. "Shep, get outta there. You just ate breakfast."

The dog trotted away, tail wagging. Without Justine's presence, maybe he'd get information from the hired hand. "Magnum's always hungry." Trey chuckled.

"Shep's a scrounge. Surprised you're still here."

"After all Justine went through, I wouldn't leave her without a protection detail."

Will harrumphed. "She has me. I ain't afraid of nothin'."

Yeah, except you might be part of the problem. Justine hadn't told Will about the first kidnapping, so he had limited information. Unless he was in on it. "I appreciate your help. Justine does too."

"Well, you won't be here forever, right?"

Unsure how to respond, Trey opted to redirect. "This place is too large for one person to monitor alone."

"Yeah, s'pose that's true enough."

Glad I have your approval.

Will's gaze moved to Shep, who was making a second attempt at the trash can. "Shoo.

"How many of you are there?" Will narrowed his eyes.

Trey grinned. "If you mean siblings, there's five total."

"Eight in mine. Nothing more important than family unless they've done you wrong."

While he had Will's attention, Trey opted to probe for information. "Justine tells me you've been helping her out for a while."

"Yeah. She pays better than most, but with all those critters eating up her money, she can't afford me full-time." Will spit. "Waste of time and cash, taking care of throwaways nobody wants."

And just when he thought he'd misjudged Will, Trey reverted back to wanting to smack him. Maybe the guy had had a bad experience with animals as a child or something. If Will had been in on last evening's danger, motive would be a huge factor. However, if Will resented the foster dogs and viewed them as a threat to his livelihood, was that reason enough?

Testing the waters, Trey said, "Though without

them, she'd probably request your assistance less than she does."

Trey almost saw the light bulb illuminate over Will's Stetson-covered head. "S'pose so. But it ain't like this place is lacking for repairs."

A quick survey of the grounds revealed several vacant areas where buildings once occupied the spaces. "Were there many outbuildings?"

"Yep. Tore down three. Course, wasn't much left of 'em anyhow. They were hazards waiting to happen. She wanted the silo gone too. I convinced her it's in good shape and might come in handy if she decides to farm the land." He pointed to a four-story cylindrical brick structure.

"I haven't had a chance to look things over, but it does appear the place needs TLC."

Will grunted. "And money. Nothing's free."

"I know that's right." Before Will interjected another comment, Trey baited him. "She's a nice lady. I can't imagine anyone wanting to hurt her."

"My granny always said your enemies ain't the folks you hate—it's the folks who hate you."

"Yeah, I see her point. Who are Justine's enemies?"

"Why ask me?"

"I'm guessing you have a pulse and historical perspective on the area." Okay, maybe a reach.

Will straightened his shoulders, standing taller, proving a little flattery went a long way. "Age has its benefits. Check out her neighbor, Richardson.

He's always bugging her about selling him this land. Been a battle since she bought the place."

"He's the one with the cows next door? Relatively speaking." Since Richardson's property sat a half mile away.

"Yep. His pa sold Justine's acreage in a gambling debt years back. He's worked hard to regain possession. More about pride than the ranch. When Justine started fostering those mutts, she won over some highfalutin folks in town. Made ol' Richardson madder than a nest full of bees."

"Mad enough to kidnap her?" Trey cast the question like a fishing line and waited for Will to bite.

The man glanced away. "Who knows?"

Answering a question with a question. Diversion tactic, or was he innocent of the incident? "Do you also work for the guy?"

"If the money's right. Gotta make a living. Folks want everything for free. I don't work for nothing."

The abrasive man was like invisible ink on a page, impossible to read.

"You never told me why you were here in the first place."

Trey debated. Was it wise telling Will the truth? "I'm working on a cold case with Justine. Found her in the trunk of her car last night after the perp attacked and abducted her from the basement."

Will's incredulous stare lingered on Trey.

Whether the man was sizing him up or digesting the news, Trey couldn't determine.

"You catch him?"

The question, though nonconfrontational, wormed insecurity under Trey's skin. No, he'd failed to catch the kidnapper. Twice. "Not yet. He escaped."

Will huffed.

"For now. But we'll have an identity on him soon." At least, he hoped so. They had very little to go off of. However, if Will was guilty and conspiring, the not-so-subtle-warning just turned up the heat.

"If he comes back, I'm ready." Will patted his gun. "Never know when unexpected danger will show up."

Precisely why Trey needed to get Justine somewhere safe. "Has that been a problem before?"

Will jerked a chin toward the adjacent property. "Trooper, if you see danger and ain't prepared for it, you're one second too late. I'd say that accurately describes how I found you in the thicket last night."

Trey studied the man. *Or how you ambushed me.*

"You two are up early." Justine cradled Clover and descended the steps. She wore another pair of khaki shorts—gray this time—and a long-sleeved plaid shirt, unbuttoned to reveal the blue tank top underneath. The outfit complemented her features, forcing Trey to avert his eyes.

"Mornin'. I'd better get busy," Will said, excusing himself.

"I didn't want to interrupt. Seems you were deep in conversation."

"Nothing significant." Trey gave his best reassuring smile.

"By the way, Richardson is annoying but harmless." How much had she overheard?

"I called Dr. Curtis, the current medical examiner."

"Just now?" Trey glanced at his watch.

"Yeah. He works strange hours. I couldn't stop thinking about the Nolans declining the autopsy. I requested he exhume and reexamine the body."

"After ten years, though, what're you hoping he'll find?"

"Proof Kayla didn't overdose. She was murdered, regardless of what the paperwork says. The question is, why?" Justine glanced beyond Trey, and he turned to follow her gaze.

The dogs frolicked around Will, who seemed none too thrilled about the company.

"He acts tough, but Will loves them," she said.

"Sure about that?"

She grinned. "Definitely. Anyway, Dr. Curtis agreed, stating how the technology developed since Kayla's death might provide something new to the case. He casually mentioned the prior ME, Dr. Elvin, might've made an oversight. Nice way of saying the guy was incompetent."

Trey mentally added Elvin to the suspect list. Had the prior ME been sloppy or paid to look the other way?

* * *

Justine had sat in numerous courtrooms under the shriveling inquisitions of merciless defense attorneys, but Mr. and Mrs. Nolan's penetrating glares were a new level of intimidation. Their exquisite home with its marble floors and vaulted ceilings was an extension of their icy reception and added to the uncomfortable atmosphere.

Justine had mastered the art of feigning confidence as a matter of survival when interviewing criminals who lived to manipulate and terrify. The same tactics applied here.

The Nolans clammed up like two oysters being harvested from the ocean when Trey introduced himself.

Ten long, silent minutes had passed since anyone had last spoken.

Justine straightened her shoulders, pinning Mr. Nolan with her question. "Mr. and Mrs. Nolan, I'd like to review the case file information with you. Were you aware Kayla feared a stalker?"

"She mentioned something about it, but Kayla always had an active imagination," Fredrick Nolan replied in a tone that lingered just a notch above condescending. He sat rigid on the leather chair, in his tailor-fitted black suit and a red power tie. His long legs were set at a perfect ninety-degree angle and both hands rested on the arms, giving him the appearance of Abraham Lincoln's memorial. His auburn hair was styled neatly, and his wiry frame was similar to Kayla's.

By comparison, Susan Nolan bore no resemblance to Kayla—not that she would, as her stepmother. Her dark hair pinned into a tight chignon and pinched lips made her narrow face more severe. "Those were silly attempts to get attention. I cannot tell you the number of ridiculous antics she pulled over the years. There was no proof of a stalker, as I'm sure you've read in Investigator Drazin's notes." She smoothed her pink dress suit and crossed her ankles. "We're busy, Miss Stark. Surely you came here for more than wasting our time with silly repetitive questions. What do you hope to accomplish by reopening Kayla's tragic case, other than drawing unwanted scrutiny to our family?"

Justine blinked, taken aback by the strange comment. Kayla's words traveled from the recesses of her memory, reminding Justine the Nolans' priorities rested on their upstanding reputation in the community. "I'm sorry for your loss, and I mean no disrespect. I only hope to identify Kayla's killer."

Susan swatted the air. "The police classified Kayla's death as suspicious, most likely a drug deal gone amiss."

"Were you aware Kayla used drugs?" Trey interjected.

Justine bristled at the accusation.

"Our daughter was an enigma and a grown

woman, Trooper Jackson. We didn't keep tabs on her all the time." Susan glowered at Trey.

Justine leaned forward. "Finding Kayla's diary was a gift, and she deserves justice. I'm sure you want that too."

"You've mentioned this diary. Where has it been all these years?" Fredrick inquired.

"I found it among old keepsakes I'd had stored," Justine explained.

Susan perched on the end of the chair. "Kayla's personal items are not for public consumption. No stranger should have access to her private thoughts. The diary must be returned to us immediately."

Justine was hardly a stranger. Rather, she knew more about Kayla than either of the parental figures sitting before her, but arguing with them benefited no one. Regardless, she'd come as a clinician. Though everything within her longed to defend her friend, she must remain objective.

"I assure you, Kayla's effects will be treated with the utmost respect. However, the diary is now documented evidence," Trey said.

Justine shot him a grateful nod.

"What makes you think you'll find anything worth dredging up the pain of the past?" Susan asked.

Fredrick adjusted his tie and placed a hand on his wife's arm. "I believe what my wife means is, after ten years without answers, we don't want to get our hopes up."

Exactly the opening Justine needed. "When I compile a profile, I use all the available evidence. Sometimes even the smallest things provide the most significant details. Anything you share with me about Kayla and those last few months is helpful."

"Like what?" Susan asked.

"For instance, Kayla's comments about a stalker and his ways of scaring her appear to reference someone who was familiar with her routines—I believe the stalker and killer are one and the same."

"You're certain the killer is a man?" Susan inquired.

"No. At this point, I can't say that with absolute certainty. However, the person was stronger than Kayla, able to subdue her, which leans toward a male suspect." Justine withdrew her notepad and pen. "Was there anyone Kayla mentioned? A coworker maybe?"

Susan sighed. "I vaguely recall her ramblings about strange gifts she'd received. In light of the drug paraphernalia discovered in her apartment, those are just drivel from an addict."

"Kayla wasn't a drug user." The words escaped Justine's lips before she restrained them. She softened her tone. "In my experience, I never witnessed her under the influence."

"Kayla kept many secrets. We all have secrets, don't we?" Susan's glare made Justine's skin crawl.

"When did you last speak with Kayla?" Trey asked.

"We've already told the police all of this." Susan smoothed her skirt again.

"It would help to get a fresh look at the case," Trey said.

"My daughter and I didn't talk on a daily basis." Fredrick crossed his arms over his chest.

Justine didn't miss the defensiveness in his tone.

"The only person who had regular interactions with Kayla was her boss and our attorney, Alex Duncan. He graciously tolerated her obnoxious personality." Susan rolled her eyes.

Justine smiled. "She was a free spirit."

Susan snorted. "That's just a polite way of saying she was out of control."

Fredrick stood. "I don't see how we can give you anything more. As soon as possible, I'd like Kayla's diary returned. Our daughter made a poor life choice and died as a result. She gave no consideration to how her actions would reflect upon us. I'm not interested in dredging up dirty laundry. I know you'd like to believe a grave injustice or conspiracy is to blame, but Investigator Drazin agreed the evidence suggested a bad drug confrontation, resulting in an overdose." A chime interrupted Fredrick, and he withdrew a cell phone from his suit pocket. He studied the screen and walked away, calling over his shoulder, "Susan, please show them out."

"You'll have to forgive my husband. Kayla's death took a toll on both of us."

"Understandably so. Thank you for your time," Trey said.

Susan led them through the living area into a long hallway. Her beige heels clicked a solemn cadence on the marble floors.

Nothing about the Nolans' home reflected Kayla. In fact, she seemed to have done everything possible to disassociate herself from them.

When they reached the entryway, Susan opened the door. Trey exited first.

Justine followed, halted by Susan's touch on her arm. "May I speak with you? Privately." She lifted her chin toward Trey.

Would she divulge something personal? "Trey, I'll be right there," Justine said.

"No problem. I'll wait in the truck," he said.

Susan closed and blocked the door. Her dark eyes narrowed. "Kayla and I were very close."

She may have viewed the relationship differently, but Kayla had called Susan an overbearing tyrant. Yet she'd striven to be the daughter both parents wanted, always falling short of their demands and expectations.

"No one was more heartbroken than I to have lost Kayla," Susan continued. "I loved her as my own. I adopted her when she was only three."

Justine hadn't known that, though Kayla had never spoken of her birth mother.

"Her death was a tragedy, and I'm sure you understand reopening this case exposes us again to the negative publicity. People can be heartless and cruel. Especially those who would like to use Kayla's misdeeds as a weapon against us."

Though Justine didn't approve of the Nolans' concern for their reputation over bringing their daughter's killer to justice, it was clear their social standing was a huge component of their lives. "I understand the media's ability to negatively affect a family."

Justine forced her arms still at her sides, though the scars itched with memories of the fire. The media had sensationalized the story of her father Ignaseus Grammert's despicable and intentional attempt to murder his daughter and wife. After beating Justine and her mother, Ignaseus set the home on fire. Victoria, her mother, played on the sympathy of the public to gain financial support, and when the attention ran dry, she reverted to pleading for her husband's release from prison, claiming it had all been a horrible accident and misunderstanding. Victoria conveniently forgot about the abuse Ignaseus inflicted on them regularly, as well as his attempt at drowning Justine once before.

Susan continued, yanking Justine to the present, "Kayla's unconscionable acts devastated our hearts. I appreciate your intentions, but the past must remain buried for everyone involved." She touched her nose with a handkerchief produced from her sleeve.

Justine chose her words carefully. "I'm sorry for all you've endured. And it's not my intention to hurt you or your husband. But a killer is still out there."

"I see." Susan's disposition changed, and the grieving mother vanished. "Tell me, dear. If it were your past being dredged up for public review, would you be as adamant? Would you willingly unveil your hidden skeletons for the sake of justice?"

Ice crystals skittered up Justine's back, and her stomach roiled. Had Kayla betrayed her and told Susan about the fire?

Summoning the last of her confidence, Justine replied, "If someone was dedicated to helping and protecting another from the same wretched fate, I would gladly sacrifice my pride to solve the case." She reached for the door, tugging it open.

Susan squinted. "Suffering is certainly a personal experience. Is vindicating a crime, even while you harm others, worth the glory you attain?"

Justine swallowed and blinked. Words eluded her. *Stay strong.* Susan used intimidation to control people. Justine had changed her last name and hadn't spoken to her parents in fifteen years. "Justice is blind for a reason, Mrs. Nolan."

Susan lifted her chin. "Hmm. Perhaps. The skeletons of our pasts tend to rear their ugly heads to destroy our present or threaten our future. It's such a shame when others' choices affect our lives in negative ways. Don't you think, dear?" Susan touched Justine's arm, squeezing a little too hard on the burn scars beneath her sheer blouse sleeve.

"How dare you!" Fredrick stormed in, face red.

"Fredrick?" Susan startled.

Justine jerked free of the woman's hold.

Fredrick lasered Justine with a glare. "You requested to have Kayla's remains exhumed?"

Word spread fast. Justine straightened to her full five-foot-four height. "The examination is a necessary part of the investigation."

Movement in her peripheral vision brought relief. Trey's determined stride said he must've overheard Fredrick's bellowing. She mentally willed him to get there faster.

"Absolutely not!" Fredrick roared.

Trey reached the entryway. "Justine, we're late for our next appointment."

Fredrick's chest heaved. "How dare you disrespect us this way? Get out! Both of you!"

"You won't get away with this," Susan injected. "We'll stop you. Whatever it takes."

Justine backed into Trey as the door slammed shut.

"What was that all about?" he whispered.

"Guess we won't be getting their cooperation with the exhumation."

Justine's gaze lingered on Susan watching from the window, a murderous expression frozen on her face. *The skeletons of our pasts tend to rear their ugly heads to destroy our present or threaten our future.* The veiled threat hovered in Justine's mind, and her arm burned from Susan's rough grip. *We'll stop you. Whatever it takes.*

Would working Kayla's case expose everything Justine had spent her adult life escaping?

FIVE

Trey's instincts blared on high alert at the Nolans' behavior, but his bigger concern was Justine's reaction and unusual silence. She'd also been rubbing her arm since they left. "Did she hurt you?"

Justine twisted to face him, hands dropping to her lap. "What? No. I'm fine. Thank you for interrupting back there."

"I've been told I have impeccable timing," Trey teased, waggling his eyebrows.

Magnum poked his head through the separation glass, panting softly.

Justine stroked Magnum's chest. "He's smiling."

Trey marveled at his partner's ability to calm a person by his furry presence. "I've always thought that about him."

"Great diversion tactic with the second-appointment ruse too."

"Oh, that was real."

Justine leaned forward. "It was? Where are we going?"

"To talk with Laslo Drazin. Fair warning—he's not thrilled about this meeting."

"Why?"

"I interrupted his travel plans." He didn't share Drazin's skittishness on the phone. One of them had to remain objective in the questioning. He'd fill Justine in on his own suppositions afterward.

Trey exited the highway and pulled into the parking lot of the large two-story truck stop. Signs boasted of showers, a restaurant and overnight accommodations. He circled around to the opposite side of the immense facility and parked in front of a wooden sign featuring a cartoon dog.

Trey lifted his phone. "We're here."

"I see you. Five minutes. That's it." Drazin disconnected.

"He's on his way." Trey opened his door, avoiding Justine's quizzical glance.

Magnum sat patiently waiting for assistance.

"Don't get too used to this, buddy. At some point you're going to have to climb down without my help."

The dog tilted his head with what could only be described as a *duh* expression.

They entered the grassy lawn and walked to a picnic bench while Magnum roamed the full thirty-foot span his leash allowed.

A Cadillac SUV pulled in beside his patrol truck, and Drazin exited the vehicle, wearing dark sunglasses. The retired investigator strode toward them. His lively Hawaiian shirt and Bermuda shorts contrasted the scowl on his bearded face.

"He looks cheerful," Justine whispered.

"That's his normal expression." Trey stood to greet Drazin. "Good morning. Thanks for meeting with us."

"As if I had a choice," Drazin groused, dropping onto the seat opposite Trey. "You're the shrink?"

"Forensic psychologist. Justine Stark." She extended a hand, which Drazin ignored.

Magnum returned and sat, allowing Drazin to pet him. "Handsome guy."

"This is Magnum," Trey said.

"Always loved the dogs. Lost my corgi, Chuck, a few months ago. Best friend a guy ever had. Great thing about pups—they aren't disappointed by who you really are." Drazin removed his sunglasses and shifted his gaze, surveying the area. "Look, I gotta make this fast. Trey told me you're working on the Nolan case. So, what do you want to know?"

"I'm developing a profile based on the crime scene and evidence."

"You can get that from my notes."

"I'd like your perspective. The file is marked 'inconclusive suspicious death,' though the Nolans are adamant it was a drug buy gone bad."

Drazin's eyes darkened. "Then you've got all you need."

Justine leaned forward. "Kayla was my best friend. Anything you tell us that might help solve her case is appreciated."

Drazin rubbed the back of his neck. "The Nolans pushed to close the investigation ASAP, but I believed the scene was staged. It was all a little too clean, if you catch my drift. The drugs on the table and Kayla's tox screen pointed to an overdose. Nothing contradicted those findings."

"In my professional opinion, prior behavior speaks volumes, and Kayla wasn't a user," Justine said.

"The case went cold right before your retirement?" Trey prodded.

The man shot him a glare. "I worked every clue until there wasn't anything left. Are you implying I did a shoddy job because I was leaving?"

Defensive. Interesting.

"Actually, considering it was your final investigation, I'd think you'd put all your efforts into solving it," Justine inserted.

That defused Drazin. "Absolutely. Wasn't easy either. The Nolans had their fingers in everything. Watched me like a hawk. Even if I'd wanted to do a less-than-stellar job—which I didn't—they'd never have allowed it."

"Losing their only daughter must've been very hard," Trey said.

Drazin snorted. "The Nolans aren't the type of folks who want scuttlebutt about them airing on the six o'clock news. They were more concerned about their reputations than solving their daughter's case. Talk to Alex Duncan, their attorney. Kayla worked for him, and he spends Saturdays at his office alone." Drazin stood, eyes focused on the truck stop parking lot, and withdrew a piece of paper from his pocket. He slid it across the table to Trey.

"Trey said you're leaving for a trip?"

"Yeah. Canada. Got friends up there."

"My dad always wanted to take my brother and me up to Alaska for a men's vacation. We still haven't made that happen." Trey slipped the note into his shirt pocket.

"Make the time. You never know if you'll get tomorrow. One more thing." A look of contemplation passed over Drazin. "The Nolans have a long arm, and you don't want to be on the wrong side of their favor. Believe me."

"Are you implying they're dangerous?" Justine asked.

"I'm not *implying* anything, because this conversation never happened." Drazin put on his sunglasses and scurried back to his vehicle.

"Well, that was interesting," Justine said. "Since we're here, I'd like to stretch my legs. I'll run in and get a large cup of coffee. What would you like?"

Trey wrinkled his nose. "It's going to be one hundred degrees with ninety percent humidity today, and you want coffee?"

"What's your point?" Justine tilted her head, blinking innocently.

He chuckled. "Would you grab a bottled raspberry tea for me?" Trey reached for his wallet.

Justine's lips curved, and she waved away the offer. "Seriously?"

"What? You thought I'd want a powered-up energy drink?"

"Something like that." The playfulness in her tone sent a strange flutter through Trey's chest.

He cleared his throat, guesstimating the distance to the store was half a football field away, and three semis in the gasoline bays blocked his view. Protectiveness consumed him.

Magnum headed toward an oak tree, tugging on the leash. Trey knew that stride. "Wait up until he's finished doing his business, and we'll escort you into the store." His attempt at sounding casual flopped, based upon Justine's quirked eyebrow.

"I don't need a babysitter. I'm perfectly capable of defending myself. No one will kidnap me from a populated truck stop."

Trey lifted his hands in surrender. "Whoa. Don't kill the messenger. Just being cautious."

Justine frowned and looked down. "Sorry. My limited sleep is starting to dampen my joyful attitude. Thank you for your concern, but I'll be fine."

Trey wasn't so sure, but she didn't give him a chance to respond. Not that he had anything brilliant to say. He walked toward Magnum, who glanced back with an expression that said "smooth."

"What?"

With one eye on Magnum and the other surveying the truck stop, Trey contemplated following her. The place was busy, so there were plenty of witnesses should anyone try to harm Justine, and as she'd said, it was broad daylight.

Still, uneasiness kept him on edge as Justine disappeared between two large semis.

Too many long minutes passed without her presence.

Disquiet niggled down Trey's spine, with a knowing he couldn't explain. "Mags, I don't like this."

"Officer, excuse me." A woman jogged toward him, waving as if he could miss her. "Officer!"

Trey glanced over his shoulder, anxious to see Justine, but there was no sight of her. He tugged on the leash. "Mags, this isn't a social call. Do what you need to so we can get on the road."

The woman closed the distance between them, invading Trey's personal-space bubble. She pressed a hand against her chest, splaying her extremely long, painted fingernails. "Oh, I'm so glad I caught you." She sidled beside Trey and lifted her blond hair, twisting and securing it up with a clip. Her heavy perfume inflamed his nostrils.

"How can I help you?" Trey shifted to keep one eye on the store.

The woman moved closer, blocking more of his view. "What a beautiful puppy. Aren't you a lovey-dovey boo-boo? What's your name, handsome?"

Why did people speak to his seventy-pound dog as though he was a toddler? "He's working." He deliberately refrained from using Magnum's name.

She reached out, disregarding everything Trey said. He stepped in her way, preventing her from touching his dog. "Ma'am, we don't recommend socializing." Rarely did Trey discourage Magnum's public interaction, but something about her bugged him.

Magnum shifted away from her in silent agreement.

"He's as handsome as his master."

Where was Justine? "We've got to get going. Have a nice day." Trey turned.

The woman clamped her dagger nails over his forearm. "But, Officer, I need your help." She blinked bloodshot brown eyes wearing heavy makeup. "I accidentally locked my keys in my car."

Trey firmly but gently removed her claw hold. "I'm sorry, but you'll have to call a locksmith."

"Please. You don't understand. A locksmith will take forever, and my little dog, Scriffy, is trapped inside."

A dog locked in the car on a stifling hot day demanded immediate attention. "I'll need to grab my window-punch tool. It'll break the glass though."

"A small price to save my Scriffy," she replied.

"Where is your car?"

The woman pointed to a sedan parked on the east side of the parking lot. It would be faster to run there than to load Magnum.

"I'll meet you there." Trey jogged to his pickup and grabbed his dual-purpose seat belt cutter and window-punch tool from his utility box in the truck bed. He turned, nearly colliding with the woman standing behind him.

"Thank you so much, Officer."

They reached her car, and Trey confirmed the door was locked. A small white dog panted inside.

Trey applied the tool, breaking the glass, and unlocked the doors.

The woman raced to the passenger side and scooped up the dog. "Oh, thank you, thank you!" She lavished kisses on the animal's head.

"No problem."

With the dog in her arms, she ran to Trey, inching too close. "I'd like to show my appreciation for you rescuing Scriffy. Maybe I could buy you a cup of coffee?"

Unable to see the convenience store door, Trey stepped to the side. "Appreciate the offer, but I'm meeting my—" he hesitated, unsure how to refer to Justine "—partner. Did you see a woman with dark hair walk out?"

She brushed a stray tendril from her face. "Darlin', I only had eyes for you. I wouldn't have seen a herd of elephants if they'd stood right in front of me."

A man came rushing around the corner, waving his arms wildly. "Hey! Get away from my car!"

Trey jerked to look at the woman. Her mouth hung open, and her gaze bounced between him and the enraged stranger.

"What's going on?" Trey asked. Had she played him?

She lifted a hand in surrender.

The man closed the distance between them, but the run had clearly worn him out. He bent over, huffing with both hands flat on his thighs. "You broke. My window," he panted.

"Liar!" the woman argued, hugging her dog closer.

Great. And now he was in the middle of a domestic dispute. "I need to see the registration and both your driver's licenses." Trey didn't have time for this, but that was the quickest way to get to the truth.

The man glared at him. "You should've asked for those things before you broke my window. Don't ya think?"

"He saved my little Scriffy-poo," the woman whined.

"What was your dog doing in my car?"

A gunshot cracked from behind them, somewhere near the long line of parked semis.

Trey spun in the direction of the sound. "Both of you, stay here."

"I'll have your badge. You can't—" the man hollered.

Trey barely heard the rest of the sentence. He took off, sprinting toward the row of trucks.

Justine's mind screamed for her to run, but every cell in her body ignored the command. Her gaze froze on the stranger's pistol, which seemed to grow to the size of a cannon.

"Get into the truck. Now, or the next bullet has your name on it."

Cornered between two ginormous semitrailers, Justine was hidden from the view of any witnesses. The passenger door of one semi stood wide, blocking her escape, and the rumble of the massive diesel engines would drown out her scream. Had anyone heard the warning shot the man had fired seconds before?

You're so stupid, choosing a shortcut between the semis instead of going the longer way around. The condemning voice echoed in her mind, feeding her fears.

No. Justine slid into the mode of a psychologist. "I'll give you my purse. Put down the gun."

"Lady, save it. Just get into the cab."

"No." Justine gripped the bottle of tea in one hand, a large foam cup in the other.

"Get inside the truck. Now." The man's thick, unruly beard covered most of his face, and the stained baseball cap shadowed his crooked nose. His bulging midsection enlarged the cartoon character on his dirty red T-shirt, stretching out the rabbit's head to unnatural proportions. He glanced past her, as if searching for someone. "C'mon, Peggy, we gotta go," he mumbled.

Justine sidestepped, fighting to steady her shaking hands.

"Move!"

Now or never. Justine took a step forward and

flung the coffee at the man's face. He yowled and threw up his hands.

Justine bolted past him.

He clamped a brawny hand over her arm, but she jerked free and ran, rounding the trailer without looking back.

In the open, she spotted Trey and Magnum sprinting toward her across the expansive lot.

"Trey! Gun!"

A shot rang out behind her.

Justine ducked in front of another rig, where Trey joined her.

Someone screamed.

"Are you okay?" Trey withdrew his weapon, one hand holding Magnum's leash.

"Yes."

"Stay here." Trey peered around the rig and returned fire.

Movement in her peripheral vision drew Justine's attention. A woman watched from the distance, her gaze nervously darting between Trey and the dog park. She quickened her pace and a husky man stumbled after her, hollering while he cradled a small dog in his arms.

As her eyes connected with Justine, she lunged into a sprint.

"Oh, I don't think so, sister." Justine took off after the woman.

The exchange of gunfire continued, as did Magnum's furious barking.

The warm sunshine beat down on Justine. She pumped her arms, increasing her speed to catch up. She reached the dog park and leaped into the air, tackling the woman to the grass.

They skidded to a stop, and Justine pushed up, pinning the woman's arms beneath her knees.

"Get off me!"

Scanning the area, Justine searched for something to bind her wrists with. Magnum rushed toward her, his leash dragging on the pavement.

"I'll kill you!" The woman wriggled, but Justine restrained her by pushing her head down.

Magnum was with her in seconds, growling, hackles raised.

"Calm down or the K-9 will attack," Justine warned.

"Don't let him bite me," she whimpered, chest heaving with frustration and exertion.

"Don't give him a reason." Justine reached out and Magnum moved closer, allowing her to disconnect his leash. "Good boy."

She wrapped the cord around the woman's wrists.

"Be still," Justine warned.

Magnum shifted protectively in front of her, emitting a low growl.

Trey hauled the gunman into view, approaching Justine.

"Wait. This is all a misunderstanding," the woman interjected.

"Really? You're going that route?"

"Honest. We wouldn't hurt you. All you had to do was go with us."

"Where?"

"Don't you say a word, Peggy," the gunman hollered as they neared.

"Who sent you to attack me?" Justine asked.

"I want a lawyer."

Sirens screamed, announcing help. Within seconds, responding patrol cars screeched into the parking lot. One sped to where Justine and Magnum stood, and a trooper she didn't recognize stepped out. She launched into an abbreviated explanation as the officer helped the woman to her feet, then handcuffed her and returned the leash to Justine. "Resourceful."

She grinned and jogged to where Trey relinquished the gunman to another trooper's custody.

"Are you okay?" Trey asked Justine, surveying her, then Magnum.

"Thanks to him."

Trey took the leash and gave his dog a scratch behind the ears. "What happened?"

"Let me start with admitting you were right."

"I like to think so," Trey teased.

"Whoever is after this diary is determined, and apparently—" she gestured toward the parking lot filled with cop cars and people "—even in broad daylight, I'm not safe." Justine gave him a quick rundown about the shortcut and abduction attempt.

"How'd you get away?"

"Threw my coffee in his face."

"Foiled by caffeine." Trey grinned, revealing identical dimples she'd failed to notice before. "Well done."

Justine shrugged. "Use what you have on hand. Magnum arrived right on time or the woman might've wriggled her way out of my hold. I borrowed his leash to tie her hands."

Trey knelt and checked Magnum's paw. A frown creased his brows. "Buddy, we need to re-dress your wound."

Justine gasped. "Did he reinjure his paw?"

"Probably just overdid it." Trey hefted the dog into his arms, and they headed for his patrol truck.

Guilt sent Justine's stomach roiling. "I'm so sorry."

"You didn't do anything wrong. Mags can't help himself. He saw you running and took off before I could stop him. He's chivalrous that way."

"Yes, he is." Justine smiled, but Magnum babied his paw, driving a nail of shame into her heart. What had she done?

Magnum shot her that irresistible grin as Trey loaded him into the kenneled area before disappearing behind the truck bed. He returned a few seconds later with a bag of medical supplies and expertly bandaged the paw. "Good as new."

Trey filled a stabilized dog bowl with bottled water. Grateful laps followed, and Trey passed her a treat. "Since you two worked the case together, you reward him."

She offered the bone-shaped biscuit and Magnum's soulful eyes pierced her as he gently lifted the treat, whiskers brushing her palm. The acceptance released a stray tear, and Justine swiped it away.

"Whoa. Hey, it's okay. See? He's fine." Trey pulled her into a hug.

She allowed herself to be held for the first time in forever. "I'm so sorry."

Justine refused to let any more tears flow while the weight of the attacks crashed onto her shoulders. She buried her face in Trey's chest, unsure how to respond. The comfort of his strength and his heartbeat calmed her.

"You're a superstar for chasing that woman down."

She lifted her head and forced a smile. "I wouldn't go that far." Her gaze traveled from Trey's blue irises, the color of tropical waters, down to his jaw, strong and firm. He leaned in, his breath warm on her face. She inched up on her toes.

An engine drew closer, and she jerked to see a patrol car approach. Trey's hold loosened, and he quickly shot a glance in Magnum's direction. Justine stepped back, arms at her sides.

The second K-9 vehicle parked beside them, and a trooper exited, then opened the back door, releasing a dog that could've been Magnum's twin.

"Who's that?" Justine asked.

"Vulture," Trey mumbled.

A smirk split the trooper's young face as he rounded the vehicle, his dog moving in stride with him. "Hey, Jackson. Out causing trouble, I see."

"Irwin, are you lost?"

Though the two spoke in jest, a gravy-thick tension hung in the air.

Irwin turned to her. "I don't think I've had the pleasure. Trooper Eric Irwin, and this is K-9 Apollo." He gestured to the Belgian Malinois beside him.

"Justine Stark." She took his proffered hand. "Pleased to meet you."

He responded with a weak single shake, then addressed Trey. "Sergeant Oliver sent us to Supply to pick up materials. Too bad we weren't a few minutes earlier or I could've come to your rescue."

Trey visibly bristled, but his expression remained neutral. Whatever was going on between the two blared animosity. "We're fine."

"Heard the call over the radio. Sounds like you had a serious run-in with some criminals. Was Magnum a help?"

Trey closed the door, creating a boundary between Magnum and Irwin. "He's staying within his light-duty restrictions."

"Good. Thought you were forcing him to work before he was ready. Would sure hate for something to happen and put Magnum out of commission permanently." Irwin patted Apollo's head.

"Trey is diligently watching over Magnum," Justine said.

"Sergeant Oliver wants a K-9 in our assigned work area." Irwin ignored Justine's comment. "Apollo's raring to go."

"Magnum's right on schedule," Trey said.

Irwin faced Justine. "You're the psychologist helping with the Nolan case?"

"Yes." Who was this guy?

"Hmm. Is today's event related?"

"It's a possibility," Trey answered.

"So someone's trying to prevent Miss Stark from testifying?"

"I'm not testifying. I'm developing a profile," Justine corrected.

"Has Jackson mentioned protective custody?" His disingenuous smile irked her.

Trey stepped between them. "So, hey, thanks for stopping by, but we were just leaving. We have an appointment and need to get going. See you around."

Irwin chuckled. "Right. Nice meeting you. Better give Apollo a quick break." He led his dog to the grassy area.

"I'm scared to ask what that was about," Justine said.

Trey moved to the patrol pickup and slid his hand along the undercarriage and wheel wells.

"What are you looking for?"

"A tracking device. How else did the trucker couple know where we were?"

"You don't think Drazin is involved, do you?" Justine joined him, working the opposite side.

"Possible. Got it." Trey held a tiny black square with a blinking green light. He flipped it over and slid a small switch, killing it. "I'll see if I can find the GPS coordinates or anything to show who owns this little tattletale."

They climbed into the truck, and Trey turned up the air-conditioning, cooling the cab's space.

"I got the impression Magnum working is an issue?"

Trey scrubbed a hand over his head. "Technically, he's not allowed to respond to calls right now. The last thing I need is Irwin reporting Mags reinjured himself."

"I see."

"And as much as I detest Irwin, he might be right. You're in danger, and although there's only a select few aware of the diary, it's obviously the catalyst for the attempts on your life. Protective custody would be better."

No way. Did he think her incapable? She'd just taken down a woman in a truck stop parking lot. Justine used her best psychologist voice. "I'm a professional, and I don't run and hide because things get hard. If I did that, I'd never accomplish anything. There's always someone out to intimidate me. All that does is fuel my determination."

Trey chuckled. "I was hoping you'd say that, but I was obligated to give you an out."

Relief coursed through her. "Want to tell me what's going on between you and Eric?"

Trey worked his jaw. "He's a new handler and determined to secure a spot."

"He's circling the injured, vying for your place?"

"You described it perfectly. I call him Eric the Vulture."

Justine chuckled. "Great minds think alike."

Trey glanced at her, then quickly averted his eyes. "I sure hope so."

"Beg your pardon?"

"Nothing. We'd better step up our game. Whoever wants the diary's contents kept a secret is willing to do anything to make that happen. Next stop, the Nolan family attorney, Alex Duncan."

SIX

"I smell smoke," Justine commented as Trey pulled onto the highway.

"What?" He leaned forward, searching through the windshield.

She laughed and swatted at him. "I meant, you're thinking so hard, I can smell the smoke burning in your brain from the effort."

Trey chuckled, settling back in his seat, and passed her a piece of paper.

She scanned the scribbled phone number and address. "Should we call first?"

"Not yet. I don't want to give him a chance to avoid us. It's only about ten minutes from here."

"Interesting the Nolans didn't recommend we meet with him," Justine mused.

"I thought the same thing."

Trey turned into a business district and approached a massive stone-and-glass building. The landscape surrounding the property offered no parking spaces. "Looks like we'll have to go in there."

A large striped bar restricted entrance into the multilevel parking garage.

"Guess we'll need him to give us access."

"I'll call." Justine dialed the number and put it on speaker. A male voice answered on the third ring. "Mr. Duncan, this is Justine Stark. I'm a forensic—"

"I know who you are."

Justine shot Trey a confused glance. He shrugged.

"As the Nolan family attorney, my loyalty lies with them first and foremost."

"Absolutely. I—" Justine began.

"I have nothing to offer regarding Kayla's case."

Justine rushed on. "With all due respect, Mr. Duncan, I believe you do."

A silent second ticked away, and she glanced at the screen, worried Alex had hung up.

"The Nolans are covered by client-attorney privilege."

"We understand that." Justine held her breath.

"I don't see the point."

"The point is justice for Kayla," Trey said.

Alex sighed. "Her death was…a tragedy."

Justine heard the difference in his demeanor. "Yes. And the case has remained dormant. I'd like to change that."

Another long pause.

"I'm sorry."

He wasn't getting off that easily. "Mr. Duncan, I realize you don't know me, but Kayla was my best friend, and she deserves justice. The Nolans deserve closure. Not to mention there is a killer still on the loose. What if someone else is hurt? Please. I'm only asking for a moment of your time." *Lord, help me get through to this guy.*

Alex lowered his voice. "Ah, yes, I do recall her mentioning you. That must be why your name was familiar to me."

Trey gave Justine a thumbs-up.

"Miss Stark, you don't realize what you're asking."

Trey opened his mouth, but Justine held up her hand, silencing him, and shook her head.

"Our conversation will be kept in the strictest of confidences."

"It's not that simple. I won't testify or go on record."

Something in his tone had her redirecting. "Mr. Duncan, are you afraid for your safety? If someone has threatened you, we can help you get protective custody."

Alex snorted. "No amount of protection would suffice. I'll meet with you. Briefly. Park on the second floor of the garage and use the stairwell to walk down. I'll turn off the security cameras there. Come to the north side of the building. There's a door where I will let you in."

The bar over the entrance lifted.

"Thank you," Justine responded, but Alex had already hung up.

Trey parked on the second floor, and the trio exited the truck. Their footsteps echoed in the empty concrete structure; dim light filtered through the drab space. They made their way to the stairwell.

Justine pushed open the heavy steel door and startled as it slammed behind them.

Inside was stuffy and dark, and Justine eagerly stepped outside, welcoming the bright summer sun.

Unlike the dank garage, the grounds of the Nolan Building were professionally landscaped, with colorful plants and flowers bordering the sidewalk. They approached the north-side door marked Personnel Only. Justine raised her hand to knock as it opened.

A bald man of average height, dressed in jeans and a navy polo shirt, stood on the opposite side. His salt-and-pepper hair was groomed short, and the goatee completed his distinguished appearance.

"Thank you for meeting with us, Mr. Duncan," Justine said.

He ignored her, glancing down at Magnum. "We don't allow dogs in the building."

Ever intuitive, Magnum sniffed Duncan's expensive shoes and sneezed.

"Magnum's got dog immunity," Trey retorted.

Justine stifled a giggle.

Alex shook his head and spun on his heel. "Follow me."

Trey shot her a conspiratorial grin, and Magnum trotted triumphantly beside him.

The hallway was painted a depressing shade of gray and ended at a stairwell door. Justine held it open while Trey lifted Magnum through, then hoisted the dog up each flight of stairs. To his credit, he never complained, but hauling the large animal had to be exhausting.

Finally, Alex stopped on the fourth-floor landing and stepped aside to allow the trio to exit the shaft. They then followed him through the darkened area, still under construction and lit by only small emergency lights.

Alex led them to a closet with three folding chairs. "Have a seat. I apologize for the clandestine atmosphere, but as I said on the phone, I'm uncomfortable doing this. This floor doesn't have security cameras."

Justine sat next to Alex, giving Trey the chair closest to the door.

"Do you fear retribution?" Justine withdrew her notepad.

He frowned. "I've been a faithful employee of the Nolan family, and they trust me. I'm afraid they'll see this meeting as a betrayal."

"How so?" Trey leaned forward, elbows on his knees.

Alex glanced down and seemed to study the floor.

Justine said, "Mr. Duncan, I realize this isn't easy, but I assure you we will not misuse any of the information you tell us."

Several seconds passed before Alex spoke. "The Nolans are prominent pillars of the Lincoln community."

Justine forced herself not to roll her eyes. She was so incredibly over hearing about the Nolans' fine reputation.

Alex continued, "Kayla fought not to fit into their mold, but I adored her. She was a great kid. Hard worker too. She had a good eye for business and accounting. One month in my office, and she'd done what the previous accountant hadn't accomplished in twenty years."

"Did you work closely with Kayla?" Trey asked.

Alex snorted and lifted his chin. "I'm a corporate attorney with enough responsibility, but Mr. Nolan reassigned the accounting division to report to me with the specification I supervise Kayla. I'm not sure if that was punishment or favor. I certainly didn't have time for babysitting. Not that Kayla needed one."

An attorney overseeing the business financials was unusual but not completely out of the question. "Had something prompted that reorganization?" Justine asked.

"Mr. Nolan is obsessive about money. Under the previous accountant, he became aware of several errors. Nolan tossed the man out before he knew what hit him. Kayla was an accounting major in college, so he got his academic money's worth in having her work for him. His words, not mine," Alex explained.

"Did Kayla locate the source of the errors?" Trey pressed.

"No, but she implemented a system of checks and balances to prevent it from happening again."

"Was the previous accountant charged?" Trey asked.

"How could he be? There was no proof he was responsible or had done anything blatantly illegal. He covered his tracks well."

"I'm confused with what that has to do with this surreptitious meeting," Trey said.

Alex narrowed his eyes. "Tell me, Officer, would you be happy knowing your most trusted confidant talked with the police about the investigation of your daughter? How do you think the Nolans will take that bit of news?"

"If they trust you, and you've got nothing to hide, why worry?" Trey straightened his shoulders, gaze unwavering from Alex.

Justine intervened before the men threw punches. "Mr. Duncan—"

"Alex, please, dear," he said in a voice smooth as ice cream.

"Alex, my goal is to develop the profile of the killer. I'm most interested in the clues available to help me do that. What can you tell me about Kayla's state of mind the week prior to her death?"

"Agitated. You were her friend. Did she mention a stalker to you?" Alex addressed Justine.

"Yes."

"Was there any proof of her claims?"

Justine hesitated, unwilling to share details from the diary. "Only gifts the stalker left."

Alex frowned. "Did she show those to the police?"

"No, sir, she threw them away."

Alex shook his head. "That was unwise. Might've helped her since her parents didn't believe the stalker allegations. They viewed them as another of her attention-seeking antics."

"Why would she need to seek their attention?" Trey asked.

"Why does any child?" Alex sighed, annoyance written in his expression. "She put them through the wringer in her teenage years. Always so rebellious and wild."

"Did she get into trouble with the law?" Trey asked.

"No, never like that. But she worked hard to embarrass and annoy them. Once at a country club event, Kayla showed up accompanied by a motorcycle gang! Can you imagine? They drove over the golf course, tearing up the greens. She strutted into the dinner, wearing black leather, on the arm of a hooligan twice her age, as though it were the most natural thing in the world. That girl was a force to be reckoned with. Susan tried to corral the wild child and make her a respectable young lady."

Justine shoved down a grin, picturing Kayla pulling such a stunt.

Trey interjected, "Did you witness Kayla using drugs?"

"She died of an overdose. I'd say that answers your question," Alex bit out.

Justine bristled. "However, that's counter to her normal MO. Did she have visitors at the office?"

Alex seemed to ponder that. "No, but she took long lunches several days in a row. Caused quite the uproar with the other staff. They interpreted it as her taking advantage of her position as a Nolan."

"Did she meet with anyone?"

Alex shrugged. "I'm not accustomed to following my personnel on their lunch breaks."

"Did Kayla report to work under the influence of drugs or alcohol?" Trey probed.

Justine glared at him. *Let it go already.*

"Who could tell the difference between Kayla's boisterous ways or intoxication?"

"So, no," Justine concluded.

Trey quirked a brow. "Were any of the employees who viewed Kayla's role as nepotism vying for the same position?"

Alex nodded. "As a matter of fact, yes. Grant Barron was so angry about being passed over, he threatened to quit, until Susan offered him a considerable pay raise."

Had Barron sought revenge by stalking Kayla?

"Look, the Nolans are very good to me, and I will not speak ill of them. However, I liked Kayla. She was refreshing in a monotonous environment and brought life to the office. Kayla was one person Mr. Nolan couldn't tame, and they fought often. They were quite accustomed to getting whatever they wanted. Mr. Nolan still is." Alex hesitated. "You didn't hear this from me, but Mr. Nolan's temper is an issue. Susan's confided her own fears about her husband to me. She said he was desperate to deal with Kayla."

"We've seen a glimpse of Mr. Nolan's temper," Justine said.

"Oh, yes, the exhumation. He already contacted me about that. Expect a motion to dismiss, by the way," Alex said with the ease of a weatherman reporting the forecast.

"Why did the Nolans decline an autopsy? Wouldn't that be a normal course of action in a suspicious death?" Justine continued.

Alex snorted. "Why bother when the intoxication-panel screening showed she'd overdosed? I understand your hope for due diligence, but let me share a tidbit that may change your mind. Kayla demanded her inheritance early, expressing a desire to travel the world. Naturally, Nolan viewed it as Kayla throwing away her career. They had a big fight the night before her death. Susan tried to intervene, but he threatened her."

Kayla had never mentioned a trip, her inheritance or fearing her father. "Are you implying Mr. Nolan killed his own daughter?"

"Absolutely not," Alex said. "Simply that Kayla had the gift of manipulation. Something she learned from Nolan, no doubt. Isn't it ironic we detest most in others those traits we see in ourselves?" Alex locked eyes with her. "However, I don't believe traveling was her intention. Rather, Kayla got involved with the wrong people, not realizing the cost."

"You think she owed a drug dealer who retaliated when she couldn't pay?" Trey clarified.

"Yes."

"That sounds out of character for Kayla," Justine insisted.

"Except I also never shared that Kayla came to me, desperate for money. I gave her a few hundred dollars, as it was all that I had on hand. Such a sad situation."

Justine wasn't convinced, but arguing with Alex was futile. Any noncash deficits in Kayla's financial records would confirm or refute the man's claims.

"Additionally, the Nolans want Kayla's diary. I'm sure you appreciate the significance of such a personal item."

"And when the investigation is finished, they'll be able to take it," Justine explained.

Alex frowned, glanced at his expensive imported watch and stood. "There's nothing more I can offer, and I have another appointment today, so I'll see you out."

Justine rose. "Thank you for meeting with us."

The departure was solemn as they went back down the stairs and out of the building. Alex paused, his hand bracing open the door. "Oh, I forgot my briefcase. Please go on ahead."

Trey shot a look at Justine. "Okay..."

Once they were belted in the pickup and Trey had started the engine, Justine said, "I'm not sure I believe him about Kayla asking for her inheritance."

"Me either."

Trey backed out of the space and drove down the ramp, exiting the garage.

A blast from behind them rocked the ground. Concrete rained around the truck.

Trey sped from the property, and Justine twisted in her seat as a massive chunk of cement landed where the pickup had been only a second before.

Dust and debris clouded the space.

Trey parked at a distance.

Justine gaped in disbelief at the decimated structure. "We could've been killed! Was Alex inside there?"

Trey threw open his door. "I don't know. I'll check. Stay here."

"No way. I'm going with you."

"If there's a secondary device, I don't want you hurt. And I won't risk Magnum getting reinjured."

On cue, Magnum poked his head out of the divider between them. She wanted to argue but couldn't disagree. The dog might hurt himself on the rubble. Justine acquiesced for his sake. "Fine."

Trey stepped out of the vehicle, cautiously working his way toward the garage, disappearing into the fog.

"Lord, keep him safe."

Her phone rang, and she glanced down. Alex's number. "Alex? Where are you?"

"If I hadn't forgotten my briefcase, I'd be dead! I told you it was dangerous to meet. Now do you believe me?"

* * *

Trey's emotions seesawed between anger at himself and Alex Duncan. Thankfully, Sergeant Oliver offered to handle the garage-bomb investigation after reaming out Trey for endangering Justine. The fire investigators located the ignition source in Alex's luxury sedan, and Trey shared the information with Justine. Oliver concluded by commanding they return to the ranch ASAP. The berating added to Trey's self-loathing for his failure to protect Justine.

They sat eating a quick meal at Trey's kitchen table before he packed a few essentials, and they got on the road again.

"That bomb was intended for Alex," Justine reminded him, invading his internal tirade.

"Except it was convenient he forgot his briefcase, disconnected the security cameras so we wouldn't have any footage to refer to and stayed in the building where he wouldn't be affected by the blast."

"What will your boss do about Alex's plea for confidentiality? If he pushes the man, we might lose any leads if the bizarre story he told us has any credibility."

Trey worked his jaw. "For now, he's agreed to keep Alex's involvement under wraps." That hadn't been an easy request. Oliver, like Trey, found the events a little too coincidental. After some discussion, Oliver conceded Duncan had a bead on the Nolans and they couldn't lose that connection.

His phone rang. Oliver. Great. Round two. "Boss."

"As if today hasn't been enough fun, the captain just advised you have seventy-two hours to provide sufficient evidence to continue working this case or you'll be reassigned," Oliver said.

Trey pulled the phone away from his ear and stared at the screen, praying he'd misunderstood. "Hold on."

Justine paused, hamburger in hand, midbite.

He covered the receiver. "Be right back." Trey stepped outside and closed the sliding glass door before continuing, "Sarge, that's impossible. This is a decade-old cold case. How am I supposed to solve it in seventy-two hours?"

"You just need to come up with evidence to justify working on it."

"I assumed an unsolved murder of an innocent woman sufficed. Not to mention dodging kidnappers and a bomb in between conducting interviews."

"Save your snappy comments for someone else. Who besides the Nolans and Duncan have you spoken to?"

Trey hesitated. "Off the record, Drazin."

"If you got Drazin to poke his head out from the retirement hole, I'm impressed. Can't say I blame him. When I retire, I plan to revert to smoke signals and will toss my cell phone into the lake before casting my fishing line."

Trey opted to cast a line of his own. "He wasn't very forthcoming and was nervous talking to us. He also left just prior to the attack at the truck stop."

"The man's devoid of personality, but that doesn't mean he set you up."

"Any word on the GPS device I found?"

"Nope. Techs are still working on it."

"Okay, but Drazin retired right after Kayla's case went cold, and rumors were he came into money thereafter."

"Kayla's investigation was the needle that broke the camel's back for him. He was already a foot out the door before it happened."

Trey grinned at Oliver's way of confusing clichés.

"What're you getting at?" Oliver asked.

No point in dancing around the question. "Did Drazin accept a payout from the Nolans to close the file?"

"Your accusation is based on the indisputable evidence you've found to support it, right?"

Trey grimaced. "Negative."

"Then until it is, don't go there."

"Roger that. I've got a long list of suspects but not enough on any of them to haul them in for questioning. Although Duncan tops that list, Justine is adamant the guy is terrified and might be imperative to the investigation, since he offered new information."

"Thought you didn't buy his story?"

"I don't. At least, not in its entirety, but he did offer details no one else has thus far." Trey sighed. "Okay, when does the clock start?"

"Already did. Captain advised he doesn't appreciate the waste of resources on this case."

Heat boiled up Trey's neck. "Since when is a murder investigation a waste of resources?"

"Suspicious death. Based on our short conversation, I'm thinking those would be the regurgitated words from the governor."

Trey paced the small concrete patio. "Why is he involved?"

"If I had to take a guess, the Nolans started making calls."

"So what? I just pack up and leave the case unsolved? Sarge, someone is trying to stop us, and Justine's in real danger."

"I don't disagree with you, but the governor's unwavering."

"Does he know about the attacks on Justine's life?"

"Does Miss Stark have enemies outside of the Nolan case?"

He'd tried talking to Justine last night, but she'd been shaken up and asked to hold off until morning. "Yes. I'm looking into every possibility."

Hopefully, Slade had information on Will Percy.

Oliver sighed. "Jackson, you and I debating this isn't going to change a thing."

Trey turned and spotted Justine reading through Kayla's journal. "The only evidence we have is Kayla's diary, but it's inconclusive."

"Oh, yes, the captain mentioned the Nolans want the diary returned to them."

"It's evidence."

"I'm aware of that. Has Miss Stark completed the criminal profile?"

"No. We're headed back to her ranch and will focus on reviewing the details this evening."

"And Slade is still helping with security?"

Trey hesitated. Would Oliver be upset with them?

"Give me a break. I know how Team Jackson works. I'm trying to get overtime authorized. Might finagle comp time, if nothing else. Miss Stark needs the protection detail, but with the upper echelon hovering like vultures, I don't see that happening."

Interesting Oliver would choose the same metaphor Trey referenced with Irwin. "We'll take care of her security."

"Keep me informed."

"Will do." Trey disconnected and pocketed his phone. Three days to solve a ten-year-old cold case. Next they'd want him to explain the Bermuda Triangle.

He turned and spotted Justine, hand perched on her hip and an expression that mirrored his mother's look of disapproval. He followed her inside. "What has to happen in seventy-two hours?"

Trey exhaled the ridiculous order in one breath, expecting Justine to explode. Instead, she gathered the remnants of their fast food. "If the Nolans intervene with the exhumation, that'll stall progress, and we can't afford the delay. We have to get on top of this and do a little preemptive work. Let's meet with Dr. Curtis and explain the urgency. Then we can use the drive to the ranch to sort through the evidence."

He blinked. She was relentless and amazing. "Right. Okay, let me finish gathering our stuff." Trey broke off a chunk of burger and handed it to Magnum, then stuffed the last bite into his mouth.

Justine paused. "Trey, I appreciate everything you've done and don't want to appear ungrateful, but you have a job to do. You can't be my personal bodyguard forever."

Trey pushed in his chair. "Sure I can. I just need my toothbrush."

A corner of Justine's lip lifted. Kneeling to pet Magnum, Trey overheard her say, "Does he ever wait for someone to respond before leaving the room?"

He chuckled. No, because he wasn't willing to leave her unprotected.

That was the reason, wasn't it?

Before the phone call, Trey's thoughts hovered around the almost kiss that Vulture Irwin had interrupted. No time for that kind of thinking now, but even as his mind raced with the impossible seventy-two-hour order and the Nolans' interference, he returned to that single consideration. Justine had softened toward him.

Hadn't she?

That made no difference. She was off-limits, and he wasn't worthy of a woman like her. As much as he detested Irwin, his arrival probably had kept Trey from doing something stupid and unacceptable.

Head in the game, Jackson.

Ten minutes later, Trey returned to the living room, duffel bag in hand. "Well, the diary is our go-to for now. Care to share what you've discovered?"

"So far, not much. However—" She pulled out the book and flattened it on her lap. "Kayla really seemed to enjoy working with Alex. At least, I'm assuming that's who she is referencing by *A*."

"She mentions this *A* a lot?"

"No, but always in a good light. Seems *A*, or Alex, was encouraging." Justine met Trey's gaze. "She tried hard to gain her family's approval, but she had bigger dreams. I remember her saying employment under her dad would be a last resort."

"What changed her mind?"

"Honestly, I don't know. She never talked about work." Justine closed the diary and gathered the case files. "I don't mean to speak ill of Drazin, but he didn't have a long list of witnesses or suspects. Gives the impression he wasn't looking particularly hard."

"I'd like to dispute that, but I can't."

"If the Nolans are trying to interfere, let's warn Dr. Curtis."

"Sounds good." Trey locked up, and they loaded into the truck.

They'd driven only a mile before Justine said, "I've debated bringing this up, but since it appears we're going to be together for the next few days, we should probably talk about what happened at the truck stop."

Trey focused on the road a little too hard, not daring to breathe. "Okay."

"I'm not trying to make excuses. Or maybe I am. But I don't normally break down like that. In my defense, I've never had guns pulled on me so many times in a twenty-four-hour period."

"No judgment here." Good—she wasn't going to tell him how out of line the almost kiss was. No harm. No foul. He exhaled relief.

"Kayla was in love with you."

Not what he'd expected. Denying Kayla's multiple romantic overtures would be childish. "She was open about her feelings."

"You didn't reciprocate?"

Trey considered his words carefully. "No. She was a good friend, and I enjoyed spending time with her in group settings. I was interested in someone else." *Chicken.* Why not tell Justine the truth?

"Kayla never mentioned that."

She'd never told Justine? Trey recalled Kayla's disregard for his rejections, subtle at first. When she hadn't taken the hint, he'd had to spell it out and confess he liked Justine. Kayla had exploded.

"I did." Weak, but it was the best he could offer.

"Oh, gotcha. She didn't take no for an answer. Kayla was used to getting her way." Justine closed the file and settled back in the seat.

Her cell phone rang, and Trey had never been more grateful for an interruption.

"Hey, Will, what's wrong?" Justine paused and gasped.

His relief was short-lived.

SEVEN

Justine's heart thudded with worry. "What's happened? The dogs? Are you hurt? Wait. You're not quitting, are you?"

"Most people start with 'hello,'" Will huffed.

"You never call unless there's something wrong."

"Quit jumpin' to conclusions. I haven't said anything yet."

Justine sat back. "Sorry, you're right. I'm catastrophizing."

"Your cat ain't got nothing to do with this."

That brought a grin to Justine's lips.

"Barney—"

"What's wrong with Barney?"

"Justine—"

"Sorry, go ahead."

"He's being ornery. Acting strange and refuses to come out of his kennel. Can't even get him off his bed to eat."

"Did you try—?"

"Yes, I tried those special bacon treats."

Barney never turned down a meal. He was the most food-motivated animal Justine had ever seen. "I'll call Dr. Abernathy."

"Now, hold on there. That money monger will charge you an arm and a leg for showing up. You've got good instincts. See what you think before you spend the bucks."

"But if he's sick—?"

"Don't get yourself all worked up. Barney ain't dead. Just seems a little down in the dumps, which ain't far for an overweight basset hound to get down to."

Justine grinned, despite the sobering topic. Will knew her too well.

"Wondered if there's medicine or something I'm supposed to give the mutt."

"No, but I'm glad you called. I'd feel better checking on him."

"It's probably best if you return home rather than staying overnight somewhere anyway."

Was that Will's reasoning for calling her? He'd never been overly protective before, but the last twenty-four hours had thrown them all into uncharted territory. "Will, what aren't you telling me?"

A long sigh. "Richardson came by looking for you."

"And?"

"I told him you were working a case."

"The man never gives up." Justine rolled her eyes and stared at the cab's ceiling.

"Yeah."

"Thanks, Will. We should be there by nightfall."

"That trooper's staying here again?" Will's irritation was palpable through the line.

Trey's presence wasn't Will's business, but Justine shoved down the snarky reply threatening to escape. "Yes. We have evidence to review."

"In that case, you don't need me around this evening. 'Sides, I've got personal dealings to tend to. Text when you're an hour out, and I'll kennel the boys. They'll be fine until you return."

Justine hesitated. "Everything all right?" Not that Will shared private matters with her. In the time she'd known him, their conversations had revolved around work-related topics.

"Yep."

"I may need to leave again tomorrow though."

"No problem. I'll be back in time."

"Okay. I'll text with tomorrow's schedule."

"Fine."

She disconnected and faced Trey.

"Not that I was trying to eavesdrop, but I take it from the conversation, something's wrong with Barney?"

"Will says he hasn't eaten, and he needs to handle a personal matter."

Trey's lip twitched, but his eyes remained on the road. "Does he normally abscond when he's supposed to be taking care of the dogs and ranch?"

She gave a dismissive sigh, not wanting to encourage Trey's skepticism. "I'd say *normal* flew out the window after I was stuffed into the trunk of my own car. Besides, I have you." Heat flushed her cheeks at the words, and she averted her eyes. "I mean, he's aware you're providing protection detail."

"I'm sure that was a huge relief for old Will,"

Trey said, sarcasm thick in his tone. "Is he always so concerned for your welfare?"

"Will's rough around the edges, but he has good intentions. However, it's clear nothing I say will convince you, so change topics."

Trey turned north and accelerated. "I'm sorry about Barney."

Was Will using Barney as a means of checking up on her? Regardless, if the dog wasn't doing well, she wanted to be there. "Poor guy. Maybe he's depressed."

"Has he been that way before?"

"Not since he first had the surgery, but that time, he had an infection."

Justine busied herself organizing the file. "It's like Drazin hit the brakes and gave up."

"Did he contact you in his investigation?" Trey asked.

"Nope. Strange, right? I considered mentioning it in our meeting with him, but he was already defensive." Justine watched the countryside passing by her window. "I should've pushed harder when Kayla died."

"Hey, don't do that to yourself."

Logically, Justine understood the words were meant as encouragement, but at that moment, Trey's comment struck her as one more person throwing up their hands in helplessness while her best friend was ignored by the people who should care the most.

The irrational wave overflowed before she could

stop it. "Is it better to pretend no one is responsible for Kayla's death? That it's a too-bad situation? Nobody is taking it seriously or dirtying their hands. Not then. And not now. We all went on with our lives, didn't we?"

Tears welled in her eyes, and she blinked them back.

"You're right," Trey said softly.

She balled her hands. Hating the way her emotions interfered with her professionalism. Maybe this was a mistake. She wasn't strong enough to fight for her friend.

"Justine, I need to tell you something."

She exhaled, talking her brain off the ledge. "Okay."

"I deserve your blame and anger over Kayla's death. I'll never try to minimize that, but please know I tried to help her. And I've always regretted not doing more."

An excuse. "Let's not talk about this any longer."

"It's the unwelcome elephant sitting between us."

As if on cue, Magnum poked his head through the divider and lapped Justine's cheek. His intrusion immediately de-escalated her mood. "You always know what to do." She stroked the dog's soft ears.

"He's great about that."

"Since you brought it up, why didn't you respond to Kayla that night? I realize she was a lot to handle at times, but she was adamant about wanting your help."

"I know."

"There were very few people she trusted. And in all fairness, she'd gone to the local police. They ignored her concerns about a stalker, especially after she told them she'd thrown away the few 'gifts' he'd left. Kayla told the officer she had a bad feeling, and he shut her down. Said he couldn't investigate feelings. Your disregard by not showing up was the final devastation."

Justine withheld her own regrets, because doing so meant admitting her jealousy. Kayla's intentions toward Trey superseded her friendship with Justine. Kayla only wanted Trey's comfort.

Not that Justine could've been with her. She'd been a state away at a conference. Would a better friend have jumped a plane and raced to Kayla's side? How could Justine know that Kayla's call would be the last?

If Justine's selfishness hadn't overridden her intelligence, Kayla wouldn't have been alone and murdered. But saying those words made all the ugliness true, and Justine couldn't bear to speak the self-condemning accusation.

Trey invaded her mental diatribe. "Let me start with a disclaimer. The night Kayla called, Magnum and I were assigned our first case together, a manhunt. We were out in the middle of a cornfield in the center of nowhere Nebraska. I couldn't leave."

She wanted to dispute his words. To attack him and blame him, but how could she? His reason was valid. Yet she returned to the safety behind the stony exterior of her heart. "So you ignored her?"

Trey frowned. "No, I sent Slade in my place."

Kayla had never mentioned Slade showing up. Justine swallowed. "And did he find anything?"

"Never got the chance. Kayla refused his help, literally slammed the door in his face."

A typical Kayla tantrum when she didn't get what she wanted. "I wasn't aware of that." *Apologize.* Tell him she didn't blame him, but the words stuck in her throat. Instead, she said, "No one took Kayla seriously."

"Did you?"

Two words that drove a spear of shame through Justine. Had she taken Kayla's stalker claims seriously? Her friend, for all her whimsical ways, did have the tendency to overdramatize. A quality Justine admired, but one that prevented her from responding to Kayla's "emergency" calls. And she couldn't ignore the omission of Slade's arrival from Kayla's story. Or was her own memory faulty?

Did Justine blame Trey? Or herself?

"You did what you had to do," Justine said, silencing her own condemning thoughts more than replying to Trey. "Let's focus on finding her killer."

The remainder of the drive was unbearably quiet, and Justine exhaled relief as Trey pulled into the medical examiner's parking lot.

Entering the building, her day was progressively getting worse.

Justine halted at the sight of Dr. Curtis and Susan Nolan conversing at the far end of the hallway. Susan's hand rested on Dr. Curtis's arm, and she tilted her head, exuding playful laughter. He nodded in agreement with whatever Susan said, their voices too soft to be overheard from the distance.

"She's gotten to him," Justine whispered, dragging Trey around the corner and out of sight.

"We could interrupt them."

"No. I don't want to gang up on him. Or have Susan lose it and make a scene. He said he'd do the exam and has always been a man of his word. I'll call later."

But Justine's instincts warned her Susan Nolan would win.

Dusk had fallen by the time Trey turned onto Justine's long gravel driveway. His headlights beamed off the darkened barn and house as he pulled in front of the garage doors, activating the motion-sensor lights.

He'd barely shifted into Park before Justine was out of the truck. "I need to check on Barney."

"Wait up." Trey hurried to climb out and release Magnum.

Justine had already reached the Dog House by the time they caught up to her. Clover did figure eights around her legs. "I think she missed me."

"For a short person, you walk extremely fast."

Justine chuckled. "Sorry. I'm a woman on a mission." She unlocked the door, unleashing a rendition of barked greetings. "Couldn't sneak up on them if I wanted to."

They stepped through the doorway, and she flipped on the overhead light.

"Well, hello. I've missed you all too. Would you mind releasing the boys for me, Trey?" she called over her shoulder, beelining for Barney's kennel.

"Sure." Trey scanned the spotless barn, making his way to Justine while Magnum reacquainted himself with each new friend.

"Hey, buddy, what's going on with you?" Justine knelt beside the basset hound.

Barney responded with a couple of slow tail thumps but remained lying on his side. He glanced up at Trey, blinking a brown soulful eye.

Justine smoothed his long ears in steady strokes, speaking softly. "I hear you don't have an appetite." She gently touched his bandaged leg. "Doesn't appear to be in pain. I know what'll do the trick."

Trey leaned against the kennel as Justine grabbed dog biscuits from the cabinet, passing treats to each animal, saving Barney for last.

Magnum inched beside Barney.

"Moral support?" Justine held out biscuits, and each dog eagerly snarfed down the treats. "That's the Barney I know."

He blinked innocently as if to say "who me?" Barney scooted off his bed and gave a good shake, jowls swaying.

"You big faker. Were you playing Will?" She laughed.

Trey opened the door, and canines burst through. Clover, Magnum and Barney took up the rear with humans trailing.

"I thought Will made it sound as if the dog was on his deathbed," Trey said.

Justine shrugged. "I think Barney may be at fault. Played Will like a fiddle."

Did Will use Barney to encourage Justine's return to the ranch? Or had Will's personal business forced him to leave? Slade hadn't found anything on the man, but Trey remained unconvinced Will was the stellar individual Justine perceived.

Which was why Trey needed evidence. "I'm going to grab our things."

Justine nodded, eyes on the meandering dogs.

After gathering his duffel bag, the bag Slade provided earlier containing the minicams and the box of case files, he locked the vehicle. Will's absence gave him the perfect opportunity to install the cameras. He set down the items on the porch.

Fireflies danced in the night air, and crickets chirped happily from the pasture.

Justine strolled along the gravel driveway, her gait relaxed, hands in her pockets. Peace oozed from her, and her smile beamed serenity. She was beautiful. Smart and compassionate. Everything Trey remembered her to be.

"I'll be right there." Justine gave a shrill whistle. Canines appeared from all directions, rushing back to her.

Trey waved, disappointed the moment had ended. He schlepped to the barn and hovered in the doorway while Justine tucked each canine into their kennel.

If he placed a camera above the door, he would have a great visual of the dogs' quarters and entry.

Not yet. She'd never agree to him invading Will's privacy without a good reason.

"Night, boys." Justine turned off the light and locked the barn. "I smell smoke again."

He chuckled at her reference to his thinking expression from earlier. "Sorry. Considering possibilities."

"Like?"

"Better, now that you've seen Barney's okay?"

"Much. Here, let me carry something."

Trey passed the duffel to her and adjusted the file box. The charm of country living and hard work encompassed the old farmhouse. "I see why you love this place."

"It has a peaceful ambience, doesn't it? I picture a large family here. Kids running around, laughing and playing. Barbecue on the grill." Her tone was wistful. "Someday."

Everything she'd said spoke to Trey's wish list too, but he dared not interrupt the precious glimpse into her thoughts. Their footsteps crunched on the gravel driveway, transitioning to swishing in the grass. Justine and Magnum beat him to the porch steps, taking them two at a time. "He must feel better too," Trey said.

Justine stumbled forward, and Trey caught and steadied her. "Careful."

"Clumsy me." She bent and inspected a board. "Another thing to add to Will's list."

Instinct had the hairs on Trey's neck rising, and he set down the stuff. "Let me clear the house before you enter."

"Don't be silly. It's an old house and boards are always lifting." Justine stood and gripped the screen door handle. She tugged it open, and Trey held it with his foot while she inserted her key.

A soft click sounded.

Trey snagged Justine, falling backward onto the porch floor, shoving Magnum with them.

The screen door slammed shut.

An explosion of wood and debris rained down.

Heart thundering against his rib cage, Trey turned, Justine still wrapped in his arms.

A large hole gaped in the center of the front door, and the screen hung by one hinge.

Magnum rushed to Trey, licking his face. "We're okay, Mags." He released Justine.

"What happened?" She scooted to a sitting position, arms around her knees.

"Wait. Keep low." Trey got to his feet. "Mags, stay."

The dog moved protectively beside Justine.

Trey withdrew his gun and flattened his back against the wall. He kicked open the remnants of the door.

A shotgun swung, suspended from the ceiling, its barrel aimed at Trey.

"Stay here while I clear the house."

Justine nodded.

Trey swept through each room on the main floor, then the basement, moving swiftly. His pulse thundered in his ears. Finally, he climbed the stairs to the upper level and paused outside Justine's closed bedroom door.

Once more, he flattened against the wall.

Gripped the knob.

And, with a fortifying breath, shoved open the door.

Silence.

Trey reached around the corner and flipped on the light switch. A soft glow emanated from the overhead fixture, filling the room.

Something blazed by Trey's face.

He ducked and swatted at it.

The object fluttered to the floor.

Trey inspected the small black bat. A laugh escaped his nervous lips. He rushed to the bathroom and grabbed a trash can to trap the creature. "I'll be back for you in a minute."

He returned to the bedroom, where the queen bed, white side table and a large oval colorful braided rug took up most of the tidy area. The door to the closet was open, and Trey quickly cleared it. Nothing beyond the bat was out of order.

Exhaling relief, Trey finished the upper level and walked to the living room.

Justine stood inspecting the gaping hole in her front door. "I can't believe this."

"I need a piece of cardboard."

Justine quirked an eyebrow. "I think wood might be a better repair."

He laughed. "No, for the bat in your bedroom."

"Thought you were going to say *belfry*. Wait. Did you say a bat?" She shivered. "Gross."

Trey followed her into the kitchen, and they cut a portion of cardboard from a box in her pantry. "Be right back."

He jogged to the second floor, slid the cardboard under the trash can, creating a seal, and hauled the unwanted visitor outside, freeing him.

Trey returned to the empty living room and walked to where a light streamed from the back room. Justine removed files from the box.

"Our batty friend is gone."

"Thank you. I don't like them, but the poor thing must've gotten trapped in my room. I'd like to say that's a new development, but I'm afraid the attic needs repairs, and in the meantime, those creatures seem to find their way inside. Another addition for Will's list."

Trey leaned against the desk. "Convenient Will was called away for personal business tonight."

Justine spun and pinned him with a glare. "Why would Will set up a snare gun?"

That was the hardest question to answer. "Okay, who did?"

"I don't know, but it had to have happened after Will left."

"Any other visitors?"

"Mr. Richardson came by looking for me, but I told you, he's harmless."

"He wants this land. That's motive."

"But why now?"

Exactly. Will was the best suspect. "How did the person know Will wouldn't be here?"

Justine shrugged. "Maybe they assumed he'd gone to bed."

She had an answer for everything, but Trey remained suspicious. "I'm just saying look at the evidence objectively."

"I need to call Will." She withdrew her phone. "He's not answering. Must be asleep."

"Or wondering why you're not dead," Trey inserted.

"Stop. I told you. Will wouldn't do that." A shrill ring interrupted them. "It's Will."

"Ask him about anything unusual and put it on speakerphone," Trey insisted.

Justine frowned but did as he asked.

"Sorry, I was busy. Is something wrong?" Will's voice sounded genuinely concerned, but Trey had heard better actors.

"Yes!" Justine launched into a speedy explanation of the snare gun.

Will grumbled a few choice words, most of which were unclear. "I left when I got your text. How'd someone get into your house to set it up?"

"Was there anything out of the ordinary today?" Justine pressed.

"Nothing except Richardson's visit."

Justine's shoulders slumped.

Trey focused on her expression. Was this a regular occurrence? Had she filed harassment charges on the neighbor? He fought the urge to speak, not wanting to stifle Will. Better if he thought Trey wasn't listening in.

"I'll head back tonight," Will assured her.

"No. It'll be fine. Trey's here."

"Oh, good to hear *Trey's* on the watch," Will snapped.

"See you in the morning?" Justine asked.

"Yep."

They disconnected, and she faced Trey. "Is this ever going to end?"

"Let's talk about Richardson. Does he threaten you?"

Justine sighed. "Never."

They walked out to the living room.

"Would he go to this extreme?" Trey slipped on a pair of latex gloves from his uniform pocket, took several pictures with his phone, then carefully removed the gun.

"No. He prefers incentives. Killing me is a little excessive, don't you think?" Exhaustion showed on her face.

"Go rest. I'll work on repairing the door."

"It'll go faster if we do it together."

Rather than argue, Trey followed Justine to the garage to gather supplies. They worked in tandem to cover the hole.

"It's not pretty, but it'll do for now. I'll order a new door tomorrow," Justine said.

Trey placed his hand on her shoulder. "I'm sorry you're going through this."

Justine nodded. "It's overwhelming."

"Would you allow me to take a few preventative measures?"

She tilted her head. "Like?"

Trey removed the cameras from the bag. "We'll place them strategically, with views of the house and barn giving you 24/7 surveillance." He held his breath, ready for her to argue.

"That's a great idea."

He blinked. Had he misunderstood?

Justine smiled. "What?"

"I'll set them up." Working quickly, Trey assembled the small cameras and placed them over the barn and both house doors.

He booted up his laptop and sat on the porch swing, checking the links to ensure they all worked.

Justine dropped beside him, the sweet smell

of lavender wafting from her. "Wow, those work great."

"Yep, and they're adjustable to focus on other areas too." Trey demonstrated the features. "The software will also record, so you can reference it later."

She leaned closer to the screen, and Trey fought the urge to inhale deeply. "I love this. Wish I'd thought to do this a long time ago. Although, I'm sure Will won't fully appreciate us watching him."

Trey moved the mouse, shifting the barn camera to face the door and kennels. "There. Now we're not invading Will's privacy."

"You're brilliant."

"Don't tell my boss. He'll expect me to work harder."

Justine chuckled. "We should tell Will though."

"Do me a favor and wait on that."

"Trey—"

"Please. See what the footage captures first. If I'm wrong, I'll buy the man a brand-new Stetson."

She grinned at him. "Fair enough. Thank you for doing this. I only wish we'd had them installed when whoever did that was here." She gestured toward the door. Her phone rang, and Justine rushed inside to grab it. "Hey, Will." She frowned. "No problem. Tomorrow afternoon is fine. Good night." Justine addressed Trey. "Will can't get a ride here until later."

Convenient. Trey called Slade, keeping near to Justine.

"Hey, everything all right?" Slade asked.

Trey explained the snare-gun incident. "Did you see anything out of the ordinary?"

"Negative. I've watched the perimeter and saw nothing more exciting than a cow in the pasture. Who could've rigged that up in the time between Will's departure and your arrival?"

He chose his words carefully, opting for the ten code on criminal history. "Exactly. Did you run the 10-29?"

"Yep. Nothing. Percy's a drifter, seems to bounce between locations in the area, but that's not a crime. I can't see him doing that, can you? It's too close, makes him suspect number one."

Trey frowned. If Will wasn't behind the attacks, who was?

EIGHT

The dead keep their secrets, and in a while, we shall be as wise as they—and as taciturn. Justine recognized Alexander Smith's quote inscribed inside the diary cover. The apropos message propelled her quest. Kayla had something to tell her, and she'd find a way to decipher it. The familiar shroud of guilt hovered over her for invading the sacred pages.

"Have you been up all night?"

She startled at Trey's entrance and glanced toward her office window, where the sun crested the horizon. "I couldn't sleep, so I was going over the evidence. Listen to this." Justine read the quote to Trey. "I can't help but wonder if she anticipated her death."

Justine wrapped and unwrapped the book's leather strap around her finger. "Here again, she says 'He's following me. Today I found a black rose—'"

"That would prove someone had been in her home. The police should've followed up."

"They probably would've if she hadn't tossed it in the trash. Regardless, a rose isn't a death threat. It's an intimidation technique. Everything points to Kayla knowing her killer. No forced entry, nothing stolen from her apartment and Kayla hated roses." Justine made a note in her notebook and took a sip of coffee. "It was a warning."

"About what? An enemy or a friend?" Trey slid onto the desk.

"Most murders are committed by people the victim knows," Justine advised.

"True." Trey walked to the evidence board hanging on the wall and seemed to study the haphazardly tacked-up Post-it Notes, her sketch of the kidnapper and a few quotes from Kayla's diary. He gave a low whistle. "Impressive. And since I'm apparently several hours behind you in working, care to walk me through what you've found so far?"

Justine moved closer, the diary in hand. "There's not much to go off, but I've managed with less."

"That's good news. We could break this down into—"

"No offense, but I use a methodology."

"I'm all ears."

Justine grinned while respectfully disagreeing. Trey Jackson was far more than just ears.

His flawless appearance showed no traces of sleeping squished on her couch, as if he'd folded himself into a drawer and unfolded again this morning. Ironically, the same could be said of Trey's return to her life. Between him and the diary, she was getting a double dose of facing the past.

A very handsome part of her past.

Trey's dark hair and blue eyes shadowed by thick lashes gave him a boyish appearance, but his stature and physique emphasized a commanding presence—the ultimate blend. Worse, he was kind, brave and thoughtful. The combination reminded Justine of the long-ago feelings she'd tucked away when Kayla first confessed her crush on Trey. Best friends didn't overstep those boundaries.

Even after one of them was gone.

His presence might put her on the precipice of confronting her own long-term issues, but it certainly wasn't unpleasant. In fact, though she'd never admit it to anyone, she was starting to enjoy being with him. She'd forgotten how charming Trey could be and how adorable those dimples were when he smiled.

"What?" Trey blinked. "Why are you looking at me like that?" He swiped a hand over his head, drawing attention to his well-defined bicep.

She glanced away and gave herself a mental slap. Not the time. Place. Or person. "Sorry, lack of sleep and I zoned out. Right. Methodology. Simply put, we assess how the murder occurred, why someone wanted Kayla dead, and that will tell us who."

"If you'd told me that prior to your kidnapping attempts, I'd have conceded Kayla's murder was a random drug buy gone bad. Wrong-place-at-the-wrong-time type of situation. But I think we've surpassed that."

"What if Kayla was overdosed against her will? I never saw her ingest anything wilder than Tabasco sauce. If my theory is correct, surely Dr. Curtis's new exam will confirm a struggle." Except Dr. Curtis still hadn't returned her call.

Trey nodded. "This is a lot of discussion prior to caffeine consumption though."

Justine laughed. "I have a single-serve coffee maker. Help yourself. Pods are beside it."

He scurried out of the room, and Justine focused on the evidence board. Within a few minutes, Trey returned, mug in hand. "Now I can function. However, you're not going to like what I'm about to say."

"I love when people start out conversations that way."

He chuckled. "I don't disagree with your exhumation idea, but the Kayla I knew was a little unconventional."

Justine grinned. "That's putting it mildly. Kayla's personality filled a room before she entered. She was uninhibited. Daring. Fearless."

Unlike me.

Kayla's openness was a strength Justine didn't possess and everything she wanted to be. "I admired her." The confession surprised Justine. Why share that?

"How can you be certain she never used?"

Justine shrugged. "Experience and faith. If Kayla's death is the result of an overdose, I don't believe it was voluntary."

Her cell phone rang, and Justine reached for the device. Unknown number.

"Justine Stark."

"This is Susan Nolan."

Confusion mingled with excitement, and Justine

waved her arms and put the call on speaker. "Mrs. Nolan, good morning."

A sniffle. "I need to talk to you and Trooper Jackson."

"What's wrong?"

"Not now. In person. I have information regarding Kayla's death. Information that will get me killed if he finds out."

"Who?"

Susan continued, ignoring the question. "Meet me in Valentine, at the bridge on the Cowboy Trail. Five o'clock."

"If you're in danger, the police—"

"Just be there."

The line disconnected.

"At least she gave us time to make the drive," Trey grumbled. "That's halfway across Nebraska."

"It's only four hours away."

Trey sighed. "What's she up to?"

"She sounded genuinely fearful."

"But why come to us now? Why not go straight to the cops? And who is 'he'?"

"Maybe the bombing at Alex's office scared her into speaking up? Plus, this works in our favor. We'll explain the need for the exhumation and get her to back off. She could stop the stupid seventy-two-hour time limit too."

"I hope you're right. I hate to be a downer, but unless Susan gives us something substantial, we're stuck at square one. There really aren't any other earth-shattering clues."

"Kayla deserves justice. You can't just say 'If we don't find something, oh well.'"

"Then this meeting has to count. If we can link your profile to someone Kayla knew, we'd have evidence to demand more time."

Justine shook her head. "It doesn't work like that. I can't go in with the intentions of pinning it to a specific person. That's a bias all by itself. We have to work every clue fresh."

Magnum strolled into the room, favoring his good side.

"Good morning, sleepy boy," she said, ruffling his fur.

"Glad you could join us," Trey teased. "He was zonked out when I woke."

"Poor guy. We did have a stressful day, and sitting in that truck must get old."

"He gets breaks, but I could let him stay inside."

"On a hot day, are you kidding?"

Trey stepped forward. "Patrol canine vehicles are equipped with a thermostat-control safety feature. If the interior exceeds the temperature, the windows automatically roll down."

Justine rose again. "Every vehicle should offer that."

"I agree. And see this?" He pointed to the small black box on the front of his tactical vest. "If I push the button, Magnum's door opens and he's trained to run to me."

"That's too cool." She leaned against the desk, considering her next words. "He did wonders for Barney's attitude last night. Why not leave him at the ranch? He enjoys exploring the property with the boys. It'd be good for them."

Trey visibly bristled. "No way. Magnum is my partner. He goes where I go."

Justine held up a hand. "Magnum shouldn't move around a lot with his injury. And you installed cameras, so you'll be able to keep an eye on him. I'm only thinking of his best interest."

"As if I don't?"

"I never said that."

"I'm not leaving my partner with *Will*." Trey spewed the man's name as if it tasted bad in his mouth.

Justine stiffened, fixing her eyes on Trey. "Will takes great care of the boys. I'd never leave my dogs in the custody of someone I thought would hurt them. I trust him implicitly."

"Even after last night? The snare gun?" Trey gave a dismissive snort, crossing his arms. "Will is one factor we'll have to agree to disagree about."

Justine dropped onto her chair, hesitant to share her painful history with Trey. But he needed to understand. "I'm careful about those I allow into my inner circle. I learned at the wise age of nineteen how damaging misplaced trust can be."

He uncrossed his arms, the defensiveness deflating in his posture. "I'm listening."

"Simon and I were engaged for two months. I'd fallen hard for him and never considered he'd abuse my trust. Imagine my surprise when he cleaned out my bank account and disappeared with the few things of value from my home."

"I'm sorry."

"It took me a long time to listen to my instincts, and it's partly why I chose psychology. It became a shield for me. I may not do a lot of things well, but human behavior is something I understand. You don't have to like Will, but at least respect my competency in choosing him to watch over my animals."

Trey sighed. "Your expertise is never in question. I wish I saw him the way you do, but too many details point to him being involved with the attempts on your life."

"Or your perception is painting that picture. Magnum would be fine here with Barney and the boys."

Trey shook his head. "Magnum is fine. I'd never compromise his recovery. He needs the interaction and enjoys working. Being left behind depresses him, and he's already contributed immensely in this investigation, even while recouping. Of all people, I'd think you'd appreciate the mental and emotional components of his total healing."

The words were like daggers. If he thought her opinion was valuable, why did he refute and shoot down everything she said? The tension hung thick between them, sucking the air from the room. Justine turned her back to Trey and busied herself with the evidence board.

"Justine, I don't mean to sound ungrateful."

"No problem."

He placed a hand on her shoulder. "Truth is, I'm probably more in need of Magnum than he is of me."

She nodded, still feeling the sting of his words.

"I'm truly sorry for what Simon did to you."

She forced a smile. "Experience gives us the wisdom to make better future choices. I resolved to never compromise myself by being codependent. If I ever entrusted my heart—and, believe me, that's a big-fat-hairy-green *if*—it'll be after I've accomplished my goals and done the things I want. I know that sounds selfish, but Simon tried to steal my dreams. I won't give someone that power again."

Trey's gaze moved downward. "But a healthy relationship encourages a couple to work together, ensuring their hopes are realized."

Rebellion and fear swam, conjuring images of her tyrannical father and cowering mother. "Not in my experience. Relationships are detrimental. I've got no interest."

Trey's smile never reached his eyes. "Sure. I get that. Me either. Got too much to do before I consider settling down."

Magnum whined.

"I'd better take him outside." His footsteps faded down the hallway.

In one conversation, they'd gone from teasing lightheartedness to high-towered distance. Just as well. They were working a case. Nothing more.

She glanced at the diary, her eye catching Kayla's script. *Justine keeps me grounded.*

Great. Killjoy Justine and Whimsical Kayla had fit together like two halves of the same book, almost as if they'd completed the missing pieces for one another. Justine had seen a side of Kayla most people hadn't—subtle and gentle. Something she'd hidden from her affluent parents. They'd bonded over the complexities of family dramas and agreed vulnerability was an intolerable weakness.

"I miss you, Kayla." Justine perched on the end of the old wooden desk.

This was the one chance she had to prove how much she cared for Kayla.

Trey strolled with Magnum outside the window, conversing with the dog. Tenderness for him flowed through her. If she did think herself capable of romance with someone, Trey would be at the top of her list. But he was off-limits. Wouldn't falling for him be the ultimate betrayal to Kayla? Friends didn't do that to each other.

Objectivity without emotion was the recipe for a successful profile. If only her feelings understood what her brain knew.

The door shut, and the clicking of Magnum's feet on the hardwood floor announced their return.

She'd not allow another man to prop her up, because that gave him the power to tear her down. She'd come too far, sacrificed too much to heal.

Never again.

Not even to Trey Jackson—the one man who held her heart in his hands, regardless if he knew it.

"Where are you taking me?" Justine leaned forward, hands braced on the dashboard. Golden tassels waved from the peaks of the sea of cornstalks. "Isn't there a parking lot closer to the bridge?"

Trey never took his eyes off the road. "I agreed to this meeting, especially if she's got something to offer in the investigation, but we're not advertising our arrival."

"So we're hiking through acres of corn to get there?"

"I'm still not convinced this is the best idea. We could be walking into an ambush. My only consolation is the trail is wide, giving me a good visual, and we're taking an alternative path to the bridge."

"You know this area?"

"Somewhat. I have one condition to this expedition."

"What's that?" Justine busied herself collecting her purse and the diary.

"If I see anything that concerns me, we're out of here."

Justine slid Kayla's journal into her khaki pants pocket. "Okay."

"Why not leave that locked in the truck?"

"As ridiculous as this might sound, having the diary with me is like keeping Kayla close. Gives me courage."

"You're the last person I'd think needed a dose of courage."

Justine grinned. "See? It works."

He chuckled, but something in his eyes said "choose your battles." And she'd agree. After the morning's dissension, this was small potatoes. "I have to say again, for the record, I'm not sure this is a good idea."

"What choice do we have? Susan sounded desperate, and you heard Alex. If Fredrick is a tyrant, he could've killed Kayla. Susan might provide the missing piece to give us the break we need."

Trey worked his jaw but said nothing more. He turned off the road and parked in a small area tucked between rows of corn. The stalks enveloped the truck, camouflaging it.

"If you didn't know this place was here, you'd drive right past it."

"Exactly. We're hidden."

"Do you think that's necessary?" Justine second-guessed herself. Was meeting Susan naive?

Trey gripped the steering wheel. "I don't know."

"Well, now I feel all warm and fuzzy," Justine teased, attempting to lighten the mood. "Come on.

We'll make this quick and get out of here." She stepped into the towering plants and around to where Trey stood at the tailgate.

Magnum wagged his tail, rocking a cornstalk.

"After you."

Trey led the way. Grasshoppers bounced between them, and the excessive temperature plastered her shirt to her back. They traipsed through the field until it opened to a dirt lot, eventually leading to the Cowboy Trail. Trees surrounded them on both sides of the red gravel path bordered by yellow and purple flowering plants.

"This is pretty."

Trey didn't respond, focused on surveying their surroundings.

"I appreciate your dedication to our safety, but it's a little perplexing."

He stopped and lifted the binoculars, scanning the distance. "I promise to be better company once I'm certain there's no one out to ambush us."

"It even smells nice." Justine leaned down, sniffing a flower, birds chirping cheerfully above her. "I remember seeing pictures on the news about the river flooding here this past spring. It was devastating, but to see it now, you'd never know it happened."

"Nature has a way of recovering from tragedy." Trey started walking again, and she hurried to catch up with him.

"It's like we're the only two people out here."

Trey paused. "Let's hope so."

"You're making me nervous."

"Just being cautious." Trey stooped and removed Magnum's leash, giving the dog free rein. "He'd spot someone before I did."

"Good idea. How far is the bridge?"

"Probably a half mile or so, which is why we're here extra early."

They made their way along the path tucked between lush green foliage. Focused on the scenery, Justine spotted a mulberry tree and moved toward it, nearly tripping over Magnum as he paused beneath it. "Sorry, sweetie."

Trey rushed to her side and reached for Magnum's collar. "Mags, no. He loves mulberries."

Justine snickered. "Ah, let the poor guy have a treat. Besides, who passes on fresh mulberries?"

Magnum snatched more abandoned berries, proving her words.

"Want one?" Justine picked a couple, popped them into her mouth and relished the sweet fruit.

Trey smiled. "We loved gathering them as kids. My grandmother had rows of mulberry trees. She made it sound fun, but I'm sure we were cheap labor. Will work for mulberry pie." He waggled his eyebrows, and Justine couldn't help laughing.

She gathered a handful of the plump purple berries and held one between her fingertips, lifting it to Trey's mouth. He hesitated, then accepted the offering, grazing her skin with his surprisingly soft lips.

The touch felt like a battery-jumper-cable jolt, and she fought not to jerk away her hand, instead giving him a shaky smile.

Had the contact rattled him in the same way?

Trey collected more of the berries, snacking on them. "I'd forgotten how good they are."

Apparently not.

Justine joined him, filling her hands. "We could just eat mulberries all day."

Trey chuckled. "Maybe after we meet with Susan."

"Right. Almost forgot why we're here." Justine walked past him. Magnum trotted ahead. The fine red rocks crunched beneath their feet. "It's hard to believe we were fighting for our lives less than twenty-four hours ago." She inhaled. "I'd be content staying here and forgetting my cares for a few days."

"The outdoors does that for me too."

The irony that she and Trey enjoyed so many of the same things wasn't lost on Justine, but the weight of the diary in her pocket reminded her that her feelings for Trey weren't allowed. She wouldn't do that to Kayla.

Or to herself.

The path curved around a bend.

"Before we go farther, let me do a little recon." Trey pointed to a long line of trees ten feet to the right. The branches were wide and varied, perfect for climbing.

She followed him off the path through knee-high grass, the tip of Magnum's tail leading the way. Trey's easy climb up the tree made him look more like a young boy than a seasoned trooper. She glanced up and caught sight of him watching through binoculars and leaning out too far on a branch.

"Well?"

"There's a sports car parking. Susan's arrived," Trey called.

"Is she alone?"

"Appears so."

Trey moved down the tree. "She's early, so let's head to the bridge."

The trio returned to the path, quickening their pace. "I wonder what she has to tell us."

Justine slowed at the sound of rushing water. The rock path became wood and connected with a large steel bridge ahead. Trey and Magnum continued walking, not noticing her hesitation.

She swallowed against the dryness in her throat, willing her body to move until she reached the railing. Her hand clutched the warm metal, and she clung for dear life, fear rising like the waters flowing swiftly below. She peered over the edge, keeping as far back as possible, unable to take another step.

Lord, I can't do this.

"Are you coming?" Trey called, but his voice sounded distant.

One step at a time. Justine lifted her one-ton-heavy foot. Forward.

Her pulse raced.

She advanced two more steps onto the steel-beamed floor and halted. Every muscle in her body locked up. She'd bit Trey's head off at the house, declaring her competency. How could she tell him water terrified her? Rather, death by drowning.

Trey rushed to her, alarm written in his eyes. He lifted the binoculars, surveying the area. "What's wrong? Did you see something?"

"I didn't realize the river was so high," she squeaked.

Trey leaned his hip against the railing and whistled for Magnum. The dog bounded to his side. Trey secured his leash. "At one time, the bridge was under water. Normally, the river is shallow enough to walk in, only up to your knees, but this part is abnormally deep."

As if that was a comfort.

He pointed to the edges where a wall of jagged sand cascaded, leaving only a few inches between the riverbank and the waters. "It's a great place for kayaking, although that wouldn't be wise today. River's moving a little swift."

Justine held tight to the bridge, immobile, words eluding her. *Say something. Anything.*

"Not into water sports?"

She'd waited too long. *And now you've done it. There's nothing to be ashamed of.* But she refused to voice her fears, instead opting to change the subject. "This is really pretty. Except for the graffiti someone so lovingly added." She pointed to the beams marred with spray-painted words and images.

"People have to find a way to ruin things." Trey sighed, turning to face the water again.

Magnum barked and tugged on his leash, sniffing the underside of the bridge.

Justine followed closely, grateful when her feet hit solid ground. "What's he got?"

"I'm not sure. He's on to something."

Magnum sniffed vigorously, inching along the bank and moving toward the tree line. She and Trey trailed, their feet sliding on the bank's shifting sands.

A rustle in the leaves made Justine pause.

She jerked and turned.

Only the sound of the water reached her ears.

"What's wrong?"

"I don't know. Thought I heard something. Probably just my overactive imagination," she said, brushing aside a stray hair.

Magnum spun and lunged, barking at the tree-lined path.

"You're not overactively imagining anything," a man said, emerging from between the trees, gun aimed at them.

NINE

Trey gripped Magnum's leash with one hand, reaching for his gun with the other. Magnum barked furiously, straining to attack the stranger.

"Touch your gun or make a move, and I'll shoot your dog before I shoot her."

Any other day, Trey would've unleashed Magnum, but his injury might delay his reaction time. He couldn't risk losing his partner.

"Shut that stupid mutt up!" the man ordered.

"Nein." Trey tugged Magnum back and shifted to cover Justine.

Justine gasped. "What do you want?"

Shadows hid the man's face. "You're smarter than that. Toss the diary to me."

"The diary is police evidence. Why would we bring it along?" Trey inserted.

Magnum inched closer, a low growl rumbling.

"Nein," Trey whispered again.

A click behind him had Trey twisting to investigate. A second assailant stood on the opposite side of the bridge, partially hidden by the trees. The sunlight glimmered off his gun. Had he been watching them the entire time?

"My friend would love to kill you where you stand. Then your body can float downriver. Along with your dog's," the first man warned.

"We can't take you to the diary without moving, genius," Trey said.

"No, but there's no need to go far, is there? Your lady friend has it in her pocket." The man fired. The bullet zinged off the metal bridge.

Justine hopped back, bumping into Trey. He steadied her, and his gaze moved to her khaki pocket above the knee. The diary bulged inside.

They were cornered. Unless...

Trey's eyes traveled to the rushing waters, following the river into the low-hanging trees as it curved and disappeared from sight. If they jumped in and let the current carry them around the bend, they'd be hidden in the tall grass and could escape to where he'd parked the truck.

The diary would be ruined, but what choice did they have? Would Justine agree?

And how to get Magnum into the river too?

They'd need a running start to clear the sandy bank before diving. The guy had already threatened to shoot them, so turning their backs was unwise. But Justine's body language on the bridge had told him she feared the water.

Justine faced Trey. "What do we do?"

"Walk up here, lady," the man ordered again.

If Justine went first, Trey could grab his gun and cover her. At least, he prayed he would.

Right now, he needed a way to communicate the plan. "Justine, you know we can't get away from them," he said loudly. "It's hopeless. What're we going to do? Jump into the river? The current would drag us away."

Her eyes widened with what he hoped was understanding. "You're right," she said, maintaining the ruse. Then she mumbled, "I can't swim."

So that was why she'd locked up on the bridge.

Magnum continued growling.

"He can," Trey whispered.

Justine glanced down. "Okay." She gave a slow nod and turned her back to him, facing the gunman. "Don't shoot. I'm coming."

"Yeah, yeah, hurry up," the man said, annoyed.

"The ground is steep. Let me help," Trey offered.

"I don't need you. Just her."

"True, but if she slips and falls, and you have to help her, you can't do that and keep your gun on me."

"That's why I have a partner, *genius*."

"Fine. Have it your way." Trey leaned closer to Justine and whispered, "Take a step toward him, then turn, run and aim for the river. I'll be right behind you."

She shook her head. "I can't."

"Yes, you can. Don't panic when you hit the water. Magnum will help you," Trey whispered. "On three."

"Knock off the whispering and get up here!"

"Okay, I'm coming," she called.

Trey pressed Magnum's leash into her hand. "One, two—"

Justine executed the plan perfectly. "Magnum!" The dog jumped in beside her.

"Stop!" Curses accompanied bullets from both attackers.

Trey returned fire, his gaze ricocheting between the assailants and Justine.

He shot several consecutive rounds, then launched into the river, gun still clutched in his hand. Justine and Magnum had rounded the bend, taking them from sight.

Trey swam with fury, allowing the current to provide an extra boost.

The men continued shooting, forcing Trey underwater. The murky water was impossible to see through and he sprang to the surface. Algae stung his nose, and sticks brushed his fingers.

Ahead, the river forked. Justine and Magnum clung to a beaver dam made of twigs and branches on the right, but they had to keep moving downriver or the men would catch up.

Justine inched toward the edge, using a fallen tree.

Trey increased his strokes. "Wait."

She turned, eyes wide with fear.

He reached for her. "I've got you. Kick your legs."

"There!"

A barrage of hissing *pffts* surrounded them as bullets hit the water and sandy bank.

Trey pulled her toward the fork, aiming for the opposite waterway. "Keep kicking."

Magnum swam with ease beside him, and they continued downriver and slid behind a marshy area with tall cattails.

After several seconds, the gunfire stopped. Trey lost visuals of the men and prayed they weren't able to see him and Justine.

They climbed out and slipped into the brush. Magnum gave a thorough shake, flinging water from his fur.

Trey checked his magazine. Not enough ammunition for a second shoot-out. He holstered the weapon. "Stay silent and low."

Hidden in the tall grass, they hunkered down while Trey used the binoculars still hanging around his neck.

The men searched for them on both sides of the river.

He motioned for Justine, and they crept along the tree line until the men's voices faded completely.

Once more, they paused, and Trey exhaled relief at the shooters running in the opposite direction. No doubt from where they'd parked before ambushing the trio earlier.

"Think they've gone?" Justine whispered.

"Doubtful, but we're not far from the pickup."

Concealed by the thick mass of trees, they walked toward the north. Familiar rows of corn promised they were almost free. Entering the fields, they startled grasshoppers, which pinged in all directions. To her credit, Justine didn't make a sound. Even

Magnum seemed to understand the magnitude of the moment and remained quiet. Nearing the edge of the cornfield, they stopped. Trey's truck sat parked five feet away.

But was it safe? Were the men watching?

"Wait here."

Trey stepped out, binoculars raised, and surveyed the area. A soft wind rustled the crop.

Nothing.

He lifted his key fob, hoping it still worked, and pressed the button. The door locks clicked. *Thank You, Lord.*

One more check.

Trey rushed to the vehicle and searched the undercarriage, wheel wells and every place it was conceivable to hide a GPS or bomb. Convinced all had remained safe, he waved over Justine and Magnum.

They made record time getting into the cab and exiting the area. Trey used his patrol radio and called in the gunmen, giving the best descriptions possible with the little information he had. "They won't catch the losers."

"What about Susan? Do you think they hurt her?"

Instead of commenting, Trey withdrew his cell phone. The black screen of death, and dripping water confirmed the diagnosis. He dropped it into the closest cup holder.

"Rice," Justine said.

"What?"

"Put the phone in a bowl of rice. That might fix it."

"I appreciate your optimism, but there's not enough rice in the world to help this. It's insured and everything's backed up to the cloud, so I'm not panicking yet. However, I need to borrow yours to call Slade."

"Well…" Justine held up her cell, water oozing from the device.

"Probably should've left that in the truck too," he teased.

"Right?" Justine leaned back and pulled out the diary from her pocket. She placed it on the console, open and soaked. "I should've listened to you."

"I saw a show where books were recovered from sunken ships. Once the pages dry, they may be legible."

"I love your optimism."

"You're a good influence. First stop, phone store."

"Susan was in on the attack," Justine said.

"I'm glad you're seeing things my way. As soon as I reach Sergeant Oliver, I'm bringing her in for questioning."

"I hate to agree, but I agree."

"She set us up. The assailant on the opposite side of the bridge got there ahead of us or crossed the river farther upstream and walked down."

"And the Nolans are the ones insisting on getting the diary. Have they been responsible for the attacks?"

"That's my theory." Trey accelerated, grateful as the highway came into view. "I want as much distance between us and those criminals as possible before stopping. And I'll ask Slade to do recon at your place after we check the cameras."

"No argument here." Justine finger-combed her wet hair.

Within thirty minutes, Trey pulled into a phone store.

"We're a mess." Justine gestured at their rumpled clothes.

"Act natural," Trey teased.

They purchased replacement phones and ignored the curious look from the clerk. Returning to the truck, they plugged the devices in to charge, and as soon as they came to life, message notifications chimed for both.

"Trey, Dr. Curtis returned my call." Dread hung in Justine's tone.

"Maybe he has good news." He waited as she activated the voice mail on speaker.

"Miss Stark, I've reevaluated the evidence in Kayla Nolan's case, and I do not believe an exhumation and reexamination are warranted. I apologize for the miscommunication." Dr. Curtis's tone was robotic.

Justine's cheeks burned crimson. "Oh, that woman!"

"Susan's very busy, and we're about to fix that problem." Trey dialed Slade, and before his brother said "hello," Trey blurted out the day's events.

"Unbelievable. What's your next move?"

"Questioning Susan and charging her with multiple counts of everything I can find. In the meantime, would you run recon at the ranch?"

Slade exhaled loudly. "Oliver called me in to help serve a warrant."

Trey's stomach tanked. "Oh."

"You've got the cameras set up, though, right? Maybe stay in Lincoln tonight instead? Or at the house with Asia."

After all they'd endured, Trey wasn't endangering his sister-in-law. "We'll see."

"If we finish early, I'll head to the ranch."

"I appreciate it." Trey disconnected and called Sergeant Oliver.

"I love that we talk every day, Jackson. Don't whine about Slade. I had no choice. We're low on manpower."

"Actually, boss, you'll want to hear this." Trey explained Susan's luring them to the bridge and subsequent ambush.

"Whoa. Are you sure she was there?"

Trey reconsidered what he'd seen. "Susan drives a sports car, and a woman got out of the vehicle."

"But did you see *Susan Nolan*?" Oliver pressed.

"Whose side are you on?" Trey bit out.

"Jackson, you'd better have evidence before you accuse her of ambushing you. I'll call and request she come in to meet with you. Irwin's handling supply duty, so he'll be around and can run interference until you arrive."

Great. Irwin the Vulture to the rescue. "Roger that. If she doesn't have an alibi, that helps me."

"Don't hold your breath."

"One other thing. Justine and I witnessed Susan talking with Dr. Curtis. Now he's refusing to do the exhumation. At the very least, that's impeding an investigation."

"This is unreal. I hate bullies, and the Nolans are the quintessential example of bullies. I want that diary secured and this case solved! Whatever it contains has someone losing their mind." Oliver grunted. "District Attorney Madeline Hansen owes me a favor. Never thought I'd be using it on this though." He rattled off a phone number. "Tell her I sent you."

"Thank you."

"Transfer Justine to a safe house."

Trey smiled, eyes focused on Justine. Gold highlights shimmered in her raven hair. "Negative, sir. Her options are limited because of her dogs and the unpredictability of her hired hand. However, I installed surveillance cameras at the ranch. We're headed back ASAP."

"You've got a good handle on things. I'd prefer her in a secure location, but I understand her hesitancy. I hate to add to the stress, but Captain's unrelenting on the seventy-two hours."

"Yes, sir. Which is why we need that exhumation order."

"Agreed. Keep me updated."

"Roger that."

They disconnected and Trey pocketed his phone.

"Your boss isn't gung ho about questioning Susan?" Justine asked.

"He's bringing her in. Just cautious."

The diary lay on the console, pages slowly drying in the warmth of the summer sun. "Dr. Curtis was in total agreement about the examination. Without his cooperation and expertise, it's hopeless."

Trey's heart hurt at the dismay weighing down her shoulders. He squeezed her hand. "Did the infamous Dr. Justine Stark say *hopeless*?"

She smiled, but it never reached her eyes. "I'm not a doctor."

"Ah, close enough." He chuckled. "Are you kidding? We're just getting started."

"The Nolans have money and influence. They're beating us to every punch. It's impossible."

"Nothing is impossible," Trey said. "You pray and I'll make some calls. It's time to pull out the big guns." He dialed Madeline's number.

After four rings, she answered.

"Mrs. Hansen, I'm sorry to bother you. This is Trooper Trey Jackson. My sergeant, Mitch Oliver, authorized me to contact you. I have a predicament."

A long pause hung in the air before she spoke. "If Mitch sent you, I know it's important."

"Yes, ma'am." Trey rambled off the situation and requested the exhumation.

"I'm familiar with the prior ME and his misgivings. As well as the Nolans' influence. I'll expedite the order to you."

"Thank you."

Trey faced Justine and started the engine. "Done. The DA is issuing a court-ordered exhumation."

Hope danced in her hazel irises. "Thank you!" She squealed, diving over the console to wrap her arms around his neck.

Trey hugged her slight frame and chuckled.

Her cheeks blushed a soft pink. "I'm sorry. I just—"

"Don't apologize. I'm thrilled too."

"I'd given up."

"No way. We're our only cheerleaders."

She grinned.

Trey shifted into gear, his arms still warm from holding Justine. She'd fit so perfectly in his embrace, and he hadn't wanted to let her go. But the reaction was simply excitement for the win.

He had to keep telling himself that or he might do something stupid like blurt out his feelings.

They fell into a comfortable silence, allowing Trey to replay their earlier conversation. His heart stuttered at the glimpse into her past and his regret for being a huge jerk and shooting down her idea of leaving Magnum with Will.

But the discussion had established a firm boundary, and he'd respect it. Justine had made her feelings very clear. She wasn't interested in him or anyone. They were partners. Nothing more. Regardless of his traitorous emotions.

Get your head in the game, Jackson.

His phone rang with Oliver's icon. This couldn't be good news. "Boss."

"Word travels fast," Oliver said. "Just spoke with Madeline. The Nolans are fighting the order."

Trey gripped the wheel. "They can't do that."

"They'll stall, but they won't win."

"What do we do?"

"Keep moving forward. Use that Jackson charm at Susan's interview and get her to agree to the exhumation."

"Ugh." Trey hung up. "You'll never believe this." He shared Oliver's news.

"If they refuse, and Dr. Curtis is ordered by the judge, he might drag his feet on the examination." She lifted her phone. "My turn. I have a contact at the FBI, a forensic anthropologist, Dr. Taya McGill-Stryker."

"An independent exam. Great idea!"

"Exactly. And the Nolans won't intimidate her."

"How dare you!" Susan hugged herself, arms shaking. Her seething glare could've burned a hole through Justine.

The defensive posture conveyed an attempt to hide deception.

Trey leaned closer, invading Susan's space. "The

call will trace to your phone. There's no point in denying you lured us out there."

"I did not!"

Justine spoke calmly. "Mrs. Nolan, I can see you're upset."

"Don't placate me with your psychological babble!"

Alex sat beside Susan and Fredrick at the far end of the table. He wore a stoic expression and hadn't defended or denied Trey's accusations, disengaged from the event.

"My client is distraught over the reopening of Kayla's death investigation," Alex intervened. "As to your accusation regarding Mrs. Nolan's involvement in an ambush, be assured there is no way she could've contacted you and traveled to— Where was it you were at?"

"Valentine," Trey offered.

"Oh, yes. *Valentine*—" Alex made a note on the yellow legal pad beside him before resuming "—*and* made the trip to Lincoln in time to attend the Friends of Friends Charity lunch."

"And even if you trace a call to my phone, which you won't, there's no proof I made the call, which I didn't," Susan reiterated for the third time in ten minutes.

Alex shrugged. "In this day and age, anything electronic can be tapped and manipulated." He whispered something to Mr. Nolan, who responded with a single nod. "Let's end this ridiculous treasure hunt and prove my clients' compliance."

Alex withdrew an iPad from his briefcase and swiped at the screen, revealing a social media site for the Friends of Friends group. He played a video of the Nolans cutting the ribbon at the ceremony and pointed to the time stamp. "Proof Mr. and Mrs. Nolan were in Omaha during your alleged attack."

"There. You see?" Smugness covered Susan's face.

Justine stuffed the frustration threatening to explode. "Why would someone dressed as you entice us to meet up?"

Susan's lip twitched, and her gaze flicked to Fredrick. "I'm certain I don't know."

Trey jumped in. "Mrs. Nolan, we also saw you with Dr. Curtis, the medical examiner."

Fredrick glanced up. Was this news to him?

Susan gave a one-shoulder shrug, defiance in her eyes. "You're following me?" She turned to Alex. "That's a violation of my rights!"

He responded with a slight head shake and whispered something to her. She clamped her mouth shut, pinching her lips tightly together.

"I'm curious why you'd meet with the ME." Justine egged on Susan.

She leaned forward, her tone icy. "None of your business."

"If you're interfering with an investigation, it is all my business," Trey countered.

Susan jerked to look at him. "What else would you like to blame on me? World hunger? The financial deficit?"

"Susan—" Alex said.

"The audacity to drag us down here with claims of ambushing, attempted murder and impeding an investigation, meant only to smear our good daughter's name, is unconscionable! They want to desecrate Kayla's final resting place for selfish reasons!" Susan screeched.

"The exhumation is necessary and will be handled with the utmost care and respect for you and Kayla." Justine worked to steady her voice.

"Don't try that with me. Your sword is two-edged and too late. Dr. Curtis assured me he wouldn't exhume Kayla's remains," Susan argued.

"How much did that cost you?" Trey asked.

Susan transferred her glare to him.

"Now you're insinuating she paid off the ME?" Alex snorted.

"Yes." Trey never broke eye contact.

Like a serpent focusing on its prey, Susan slithered her gaze to Justine. "May I remind you, Justine Stark, disputing the prior ME's conclusions has disgraceful repercussions? You provided expert testimony on several cases with him, didn't you? It'd be a shame to have those files reopened and reexamined too."

The venomous words sucked the air from Justine's lungs, and her chest tightened over her racing heart. "I only want what's best for Kayla."

The satisfaction in Susan's expression preempted her next attack. "Let's not pretend you're concerned about anyone besides yourself. Isn't that how it's always been for you? Take care of number one? After all, what do you know about family?" Susan's lips formed into a knowing smirk.

The adrenaline rush caused Justine's ears to ring. She lowered her shaking hands beneath the table, hiding them from view, unwilling for the Nolans to witness her anxiety. The jab struck so deeply she could scarcely speak. She interlaced her fingers in her lap to prevent grasping her burned arms.

They knew about her father. It wouldn't be hard to find the details, the court records, the newspaper stories. How far would they go to keep her from investigating Kayla's case? Justine averted her eyes but caught a glimpse of Trey's bewilderment.

Her mind raced. Hadn't she spent her life helping others? Hadn't she devoted her work to gaining justice for victims?

Trey spoke again, but Susan's words blared in Justine's brain. What would happen if the district attorney reviewed every case she'd worked with the prior ME? Justine had addressed any mistakes she'd made with the authorities, hadn't she? Nothing egregious that would overturn a conviction, but it might create reasonable doubt. Not only in his work but in her testimony.

Run, her instincts screamed.

"That's enough! I have far better things to do than to sit and listen to this nonsense!" Fredrick shoved his steel chair across the linoleum floor, piercing the space with a loud screech.

Trey stood. "We're not finished."

"Trooper, you've wasted too much of my time. I've already missed an important meeting, and if you're determined to continue this ridiculous round of questioning, I need to notify my next appointment," Fredrick challenged.

"Maybe a small break would be good," Justine offered, hoping to de-escalate the conversation and desperately needing to escape Susan.

"Ten minutes," Trey conceded.

Fredrick stormed from the room.

"I hope you're happy with yourselves." Susan threw up her hands.

"Let's take a short walk and get a cup of coffee," Alex encouraged.

Justine had a new appreciation for the lawyer's way of calming Susan. She busied herself making notes, avoiding Susan's eyes, and remained seated until she and Trey were alone.

The quiet click of the door infused her lungs with breath.

"Are you okay?"

"I have to get out of here." Justine stood and bee-lined for the exit, then through the parking lot, sucking in the humid evening air.

Trey kept in step. "Better?"

"Nothing like drinking your oxygen." She forced levity into her response, but it fell flat. Justine roamed to a tree and faced the patrol office. "What if she's right?"

"You mean about recalling your cases?"

"Yes. No. It's just an intimidation game." Justine crossed her arms.

"By the look on your face, it was effective."

"Ugh. That bad?" Justine pressed a finger against her temple where a dull headache thrummed. "I worked several investigations with the prior ME. If his findings were off on Kayla's, they could be wrong on the others, as well. If they're all reopened, what will happen to those victims?"

Trey blew out a breath. "Tough call. Don't give Susan the satisfaction of getting inside your head with what-ifs that may never happen."

Justine's stomach twisted in knots. "I can live with the stain to my reputation. I mean, I don't want that, but it's the lesser of my worries. Trey, I've testified in some horrible cases. Court puts the victims through the wringer." A reel of the heinous stories, those especially involving innocent children and their families, played before her. "They trusted me. How would they endure it again?"

Trey placed his hands on her shoulders, grounding her. "First, the future of others is out of your control. Second, if the Nolans are this emphatic about exhuming Kayla's body, I want to know why.

"We're getting close to a breakthrough." He stepped back. "I'll stand beside whatever you decide. Maybe we don't need the exhumation."

She studied him, allowing his promise of support to feed her broken soul. She'd always fought alone. What would it be like to have someone in her corner? Strength infused her, and she shook her head. "We're not giving in. Outside of the—" she lowered her voice, glancing around "—diary, the exhumation is the only physical evidence we have. I'm not letting her intimidate me out of this investigation."

"I'm so glad you said that." Trey grinned.

Fredrick walked out of the building, engrossed in a phone conversation.

"We'd better get in there."

"After you." Trey gestured with one arm.

Once inside the air-conditioned building, Justine spotted Susan and Alex at the far end of the hallway, holding cups of coffee. Susan lifted her chin at their entrance and pivoted on her heel, turning her back to them.

"Ever wonder if she'd drown in a rainstorm?" Justine whispered.

Trey chuckled. "That's the Justine Stark superwarrior psychologist I know."

She grinned. "Sorry. That was rude."

"Nah, I'd say it's pretty accurate. And it's given me an idea. Let's do a little divide and conquer."

"How?" Justine worried her lip.

"Follow me."

Trey headed for Susan and Alex, Justine trailing.
Susan stiffened at their approach. "What?"

"We apologize for upsetting you, Mrs. Nolan."

"You should." She sniffed, dabbing at her eyes for effect.

So incredibly fake. Barney could take lessons from Susan. Justine forced a neutral expression.

Trey continued, "Your husband's still on the phone outside. He's a busy man."

"He's very important," Susan said with a dismissive wave.

"It's obvious you bring strength to the relationship. He was pretty quiet in there. Letting you handle the questioning."

Susan shrugged. "Fredrick expects that."

Trey put his hands into his pockets and rocked back on his heels. "You're a nice woman to support him. I'm sure it means sacrificing so much of yourself. Even when he's undeserving of such kindness."

Justine studied Susan's body language. Her shoulders lowered. Oh, Trey was good.

"It's my duty as his wife."

"And you're clearly the rock in the relationship. Pure class." Trey laid it on thick.

Susan's expression softened slightly. "It's not always easy, you know? Fredrick has quite the temper."

"Yes, ma'am. I've done a lot of interviews, and I must say, I can see that brewing beneath the surface. That got me to thinking—" Trey glanced toward the door. "Would you mind if we spoke privately for a moment?"

"Not without Alex," Susan countered.

"Oh, absolutely. You should always have your counsel present. That's why you make the big bucks, right, Mr. Duncan?" Trey shot him a grin.

Alex frowned and fidgeted with his watch. "Okay."

The group returned to the interrogation room, and once seated, Trey said, "Susan, something in your eyes earlier spoke fear to me."

"I'm not afraid of you," she bit back.

"Oh, not me. But I sense there is someone you fear."

Susan glanced down, then at Alex.

He nodded and patted her hand. "It's time. Tell them about Fredrick."

Susan's steel exterior melted, and her lips quivered. "Fine. The truth is, I did make that call to meet you, but Fredrick overheard and threatened to kill me." Her eyes darted nervously to the door.

"Let us help you," Justine said.

"You can't. Leave this case alone. Please. I don't want to end up like Kayla."

Justine shot Trey a look. Was she implying Fredrick had killed Kayla? "We can protect you."

Susan tilted her head. "Alex told me what happened at the garage. You don't understand the kind of man I'm married to. He'll do whatever it takes to stop this investigation."

Trey nodded. "We don't want to endanger you."

Justine forced her mouth shut. What was he saying? Surely, Trey didn't buy these lies. Everything about Susan spoke deception.

Trey continued, "I'm certain you're aware of the seventy-two-hour clock ticking on this case?"

Susan had the decency to nod. "Fredrick contacted the governor."

Trey shrugged. "Perhaps time will just run out. Justine, if Mrs. Nolan fears her husband, what else can we do?"

Justine tried to comprehend Trey's ploy. "May I speak with you outside?"

"Yes, of course. Please excuse us."

They exited the room. "What are you doing?" Justine hissed.

"Follow my lead."

Mr. Nolan reentered the building, and Trey scurried to meet up with him. "Sir, could we speak with you privately?"

He hesitated, then nodded. Trey pulled him into a different interrogation room and closed the door.

"Sir, I'll speak candidly. The evidence implicates you in Kayla's death and the garage bombing," Trey said calmly.

Fredrick jumped to his feet. "What? Are you insane? What evidence?"

"A witness has come forward," Justine inserted. Susan's accusation most likely was a lie, but Justine didn't add that part.

"That's absurd! I've never hurt anyone, especially my own daughter. I must speak with Alex immediately!"

Trey remained seated. "I'm not saying I believe it, but we need proof you're not involved. Signing the exhumation order would be a step in gathering additional evidence to exonerate you."

"With the most recent events, Susan admitted to fearing for her own life," Justine added.

Fredrick blinked. "She's worried someone will try and hurt her?"

Trey nodded. "We have to find the real killer and protect Susan. I know you want what's best for her."

Fredrick slid onto the chair, shaking his head.

Several long seconds passed.

Finally, he said, "Yes, of course. The truth is the sole means to exonerate me from this ridiculous accusation and protect my wife. What do you need from me?"

"Your cooperation," Trey said.

"What about the governor?" Justine asked.

Fredrick nodded. "Consider it done. Bring me the forms needed to authorize the exhumation."

"Thank you, sir." Trey bolted from the room and returned with the documents in seconds.

Once Fredrick had signed the forms, they returned to where Susan and Alex sat waiting. "You're free to go."

Susan quirked an eyebrow, her gaze bouncing between Fredrick and Trey. "What's going on?"

"I've authorized the exhumation," Fredrick said.

Susan jumped to her feet. "No! You can't do that. Fredrick, no!"

"It's for the best, darling," Fredrick pleaded. No longer the strong businessman, now a concerned husband.

"Alex, stop him!"

"I can't, Susan."

Susan pointed a finger at Justine. "You won't get away with this! Dr. Curtis won't perform the examination."

"Dr. Curtis's services aren't needed," Justine said triumphantly.

FBI forensic anthropologist Taya McGill-Stryker was already on her way. For once, Justine had an ally in high places.

TEN

Justine tucked the pillow under her head, exhausted. The bright blue LED letters of her clock read 1:00 a.m. Clover padded across the bed and curled into a ball beside her, purring.

Winds ushered in the promise of a rainstorm, whipping tree branches against the house and waving her bedroom drapes. Justine shoved off the covers and walked to the open window, pausing to glance over the pasture. Fresh air laced with humidity filled her senses, and she tied back the curtains, inviting the breeze in.

"Thank You, Lord." Gratitude overflowed her heart. They were close to solving the case. With Mr. Nolan's capitulation on Kayla's exhumation order and his promise to contact the governor and remove the ridiculous seventy-two-hour restriction, they'd made huge strides. Even Will had happily—or as happily as Will did anything—reported Barney had returned to his food-motivated self.

Things were definitely looking up.

Trey settled on the couch downstairs gave her a sense of comfort, though he probably longed to sleep in his own bed. Everything was coming together, and life would get back to normal. A bittersweet reminder that once they'd completed the investigation, Trey would be gone.

She sighed. That was best for everyone.

Sliding under the cool cotton sheets, Justine exhaled contentment and closed her eyes.

Sleep beckoned, and she willingly drifted off.

A thunderous roar jolted Justine awake, and she glanced at the clock. Nearly 3:00 a.m. Clover's spot was vacant. Probably off hunting for mice somewhere. Lightning splintered the night, illuminating a shadow near the window.

Justine jerked upright, hand groping for the table lamp. The sensation someone watched her sent a shiver tingling down her spine. She flipped on the light and scanned the empty room.

A second roll of thunder and the sky opened, pouring down rain.

Maybe closing the window would be best. Justine scooted off her bed, planting her feet on the cool wooden floor.

Someone grasped her ankles, and she flew forward, landing with a hard thud, and knocked over her side table. The antique lamp crashed and shattered. Hands ripped her backward, dragging her across the old rug.

She clawed at the floor covering, failing to get traction and stop the assault. Her hand caught on a piece of glass, tearing into her skin.

Justine screamed, but the sound was muffled as the attacker smashed her nose into the worn hook braids. She fought, trying to throw him off, but he held her down, smothering her.

Magnum's barks erupted outside the door.

Footsteps and a knock. "Justine, are you okay?"
Trey, help me!

Stars danced in front of her eyes, and she flailed, desperate for air.

The assailant's hand threaded through Justine's hair. He yanked back her head, restricting her cry.

"You should've walked away." He breathed against her ear, then slapped tape over her mouth. A sting in her arm sent a cold tingle oozing through her veins.

Justine jerked, and something toppled to the ground.

He cursed. "No matter. I got enough injected to shut you up."

Dizziness consumed Justine, and her mouth numbed.

The room spun, blurring her surroundings. Her arms were heavy, impossible to move.

"Figuring it out now?" The intruder cackled, something oddly familiar in his tone. He stayed behind Justine. "Don't worry. You'll be wide-awake to enjoy your demise."

"Justine?" Trey knocked again.

In one swift motion, the man hefted Justine, then tossed her onto the bed. He rolled her over and pulled the sheet to her chin, tucking her in. Darkness and a black balaclava disguised his face. "Sweet dreams."

Movement around the room ratcheted up her terror.

And then she smelled it.

Gasoline.

Justine turned her head, heard the splash of liquid hitting the floor.

Oh, Lord, no! Help me!

"Justine!" A thud against the door.

The intruder sat on the windowsill. "He won't get in to save you." A flash of lightning silhouetted his terrifying presence.

Thunder crashed, just as the man dropped the match, igniting the trail of gasoline. Like a speeding race car, the blaze zipped from the window to the door.

Frantic, Justine tried to roll, willing her body to move, but the quicksand of her bed held her down.

"Justine!"

Three repetitive thuds.

Smoke filled the space, burning her lungs.

A macabre dance of orange flames engulfed the room, a juxtaposition to the torrential downpour outside.

And the memories came crashing in, surrounding her with their terrifying claws. Dragging her back to the night of her father's attempt to kill her and her mother.

But then, rescue had come in time.

Tonight, she would die.

"Justine! Hang on!" Trey called through the fog in her mind.

"Hang on," a voice repeated, sounding so much

like sweet Mrs. Scranton, the brave neighbor who'd pulled her from the inferno.

The woman who'd rescued Justine not just from the flames but from her nightmare childhood.

But Mrs. Scranton wasn't here now.

Smoke stung her eyes, and she squeezed them shut. *Lord, fight for me.*

The heat intensified around her.

"Magnum, stay back!"

Strong arms lifted her. She was flying.

Then moving swiftly. Justine couldn't open her eyes.

"I'm here. I'm here." Trey's voice carried to her.

Water splashed onto her face, and she sucked in a breath.

Painful coughs racked her body. Trey rolled her to the side, and she wheezed, gasping. Her lungs fought against the smoke's intrusion.

"Are you okay?" Trey leaned closer. "Can you sit up?"

Justine blinked, rain cascading down her face. Unable to move, she watched the long wisps of fire reach out from her bedroom window.

"Send rescue. Structure fire, one party injured," Trey said. "Help's on the way. There's—"

Barking in the distance. Justine turned her head and spotted flames from the Dog House.

Trey was already running across the property.

This wasn't happening.

Her boys! Justine forced her energy into moving

her hand, finally gaining a weak response from her fingers. The progress infused her with hope.

Frantic barks from the Dog House tore at her heart.

Were they okay? *Lord, help Trey!*

She couldn't see him, and he'd been gone too long.

Where was Will?

Tingling returned to her hands, and Justine groped at the wet ground, nails grazing the grass and digging into the dirt beneath. The fire danced into the night air, stretching too close to the tree beside the house. She forced herself up and crawled across the lawn.

Six canines and Clover bounded toward her, then smothered Justine in a flurry of licks, wagging tails and the comfort of wet dog smell.

Trey rushed back to her side. "They're all okay. Can you stand?"

"Will," she gasped in reply.

Trey helped her up on wobbly legs. He braced her with an arm around her waist. "Will." She coughed.

"He wasn't in the building. In fact, he's nowhere to be found." The accusation in Trey's tone struck a fresh wound to her heart.

Will wouldn't do this.

Would he?

Sirens screamed in the distance, and the strobing lights of the fire truck and ambulance added to the fire's radiance. The rescue vehicles pulled onto the property. Trey hoisted her into his arms, running for the two medics who'd burst from the rig.

"I think she's been injected with something. She's struggling to move and speak." Trey placed her onto the stretcher as a female paramedic leaned in.

The woman ran her hands over Justine's arm. "I see a puncture wound. Ma'am, do you know what you were injected with?"

Justine shook her head.

"We need to get her to the hospital."

No. She couldn't leave the ranch. Her boys. "No!" Justine said, startling herself. "It's. Wearing. Off," she stammered.

Trey corralled the dogs, securing their leashes. He moved them away from the burning buildings.

Justine gaped at the fire raging all around her.

Would the nightmare ever end?

Trey stood beside the garage. A mixture of fury, self-disdain and sorrow weighed down his shoulders.

A firefighter approached. Trey tried to remember his name but came up blank.

"It's clear. We restricted the flames to the bedroom where they started, but there will be smoke and water damage throughout the house. Once daylight hits, the fire marshal will come and check it out."

"It's arson," Trey said.

"Yep, accelerant marks around the bedroom

prove that. Miss Stark is refusing to go to the hospital." He gestured to where Justine sat on the lawn, gaping at the house.

"Somehow, that doesn't surprise me." Trey shook the man's hand. "Thanks for everything."

Trey surveyed the damage as the firefighters and paramedics exited the property. Thankfully, the rains had helped stave off the flames, but the structures appeared badly damaged, and his heart hurt for Justine. Wet ash and soot lingered in the air, mingling with the fresh smell after the storm.

The constant condemning thoughts battled for attention. How had he let this happen? Who would do this?

He'd fallen asleep, but not before doing a full walk-through of the home and surrounding buildings. How had he not heard the intruder? Even Magnum hadn't warned him. Had the interloper been inside the entire time, waiting? Or had Magnum not reacted because he was familiar with the man?

And if that was the case, Will topped his suspect list. Trey had issued a BOLO for Will, who'd mysteriously disappeared after they'd spoken last night.

Fury boiled his blood.

The sun would rise soon, and they'd determine the full extent of the loss. And their next steps.

Justine walked toward him, caressing Clover and accompanied by all five rescue dogs, keeping watch over their rescuer.

"Hey. Feeling better?"

Justine shrugged. "Whatever the jerk injected me with wore off quickly. The paramedic said he must've missed or failed to get it all inside the vein. Still no sign of Will?"

"No, but are you really surprised?" Trey bit his tongue. Now wasn't the time. Once he pulled up the cameras, he'd have the proof against Will to convince Justine.

The rescue rigs disappeared from sight.

"Why would someone do this? Don't answer that. I'm sure it's pretty obvious." Justine turned to Trey's pickup. "If you hadn't suggested locking the diary in your toolbox last night, it would've been destroyed."

Perfect segue. Trey rushed to the truck, dropping the tailgate and entering the code on the lockbox. Justine joined him, and Trey tugged open the drawer, withdrawing the damp book. "Good thing you remembered. It still needs to air out."

She took the diary, holding it gingerly. "I need to keep the pages separated so they don't dry together. Let's go inside and see if there's anything salvageable from the case files."

"Let me grab my laptop."

Justine waited beside the porch steps, apprehension in her expression.

"Ready?"

They moved through the house, Justine's footsteps slowing as they entered the hallway, then walked into the back room, directly below her bedroom. Soot and water dripped from the ceiling. The files were saturated, along with Justine's evidence board.

Trey collected the box, and they went outside. "We'd better head to a hotel."

Justine's laugh held bitterness. "And what hotel is going to take my five dogs and overfed cat?" She gestured to the menagerie. "I'm not leaving."

"You can't stay in there." Trey pointed to the house.

"It's almost daylight. Not as if I'll get a ton of sleep. We can sit out here." Justine slid onto the porch swing.

The sun peeked over the horizon, filling the sky with streaks of orange and blue.

Dropping beside her, Trey placed his laptop on his legs and logged in. "Maybe the cameras caught the perp."

He focused first on the house cameras.

"Got him." Justine leaned closer to the laptop and pointed to a shadow slinking near the side of the house. "He avoids the cameras, as if he knows they're there."

Trey shifted to the barn's vantage point. If he caught Will sneaking out of the structure, Justine would have to believe him. The video showed Will entering the outbuilding around midnight, after they'd parted for the evening. Then the screen went black and remained off.

"Did someone disconnect the camera?" Justine asked.

"Someone who knew it was there," Trey clarified, selecting the footage to before they'd returned to the ranch. He watched with the intensity of a starving hawk.

The screen came to life, revealing Will sitting on the countertop in the barn. His cell rang. "What? I'm working. I'll get the money. Just need a little more time."

He sighed and stuffed the phone into his pocket.

Justine met Trey's eyes.

Motive.

They continued watching as Will walked to each kennel, grumbling as he opened the doors, leaving Barney for last.

Trey gripped the laptop's edge. If he hurt that dog...

"Boys, I'm in a mess. Y'all are the only friends I have." Will dropped to the floor beside Barney, and the other canines surrounded him. "Nobody wants to employ an old codger full-time, but I can't make it on these side jobs. I need to move and find real work, but how am I s'posed to up and leave Justine? She needs my help."

Barney whined and thumped his tail.

"You understand what it's like, being unwanted, don't ya, boy?" Will leaned against the wall and closed his eyes. "Lord, You're our Provider. Please make a way for me and Justine. Even that annoying cop friend of hers. Justine's trying hard to be a light in a dark world. Bless her, Lord, and somehow allow me to be here for her. I'm grateful You're using an old homeless man."

Trey paused the video, loath to speak the words Justine deserved to hear. "I might've been wrong about Will."

Justine's eyes shone with satisfaction. "Humility is a wonderful trait." She sobered. "Will's not the monster you labeled him, but it doesn't explain where he is."

Why would Will disappear? Or had the intruder gotten to him? He thought about the tree house incident. Was Will in danger?

"Let's check out the Dog House." Trey set down his laptop and led the way to the barn.

The door had been removed by the firefighters, and it, like the house, dripped wet from the fire hoses. The dogs wandered in, sniffing around the room.

"Trey, look!" Justine pointed to Will's accommodations. His bed was unmade, and his boots were beside the bed. "Will's in trouble. He'd never leave without his boots, or that."

They rushed to the black Stetson lying on the floor.

"Magnum." The dog moved obediently to Trey's side. He held out the hat and boots. "Track."

Magnum sniffed both and shot out the door, forcing Trey and Justine to jog to catch up. The Malinois scurried through the property to the old brick silo, circling the building several times, then poked his head through one of the square open spaces. He dropped to a sit and barked.

"He's alerting!" Justine cried.

Using his phone's flashlight app, Trey illuminated the inside of the silo. A familiar form lay still on the ground. "Will!"

Trey squeezed through the space and moved to Will's side. A big gash on his head bled profusely, but his pulse was strong. "We'll have to work together to get him out of here."

Trey gently lifted him and walked to the windows. He and Justine shimmied Will through and lowered him to the ground.

Will groaned.

"He's coming to." Justine ran to the garage and returned with a first-aid kit to cleanse the wound.

"What happened?" Will asked groggily.

"I was going to ask the same question," Trey said.

Will blinked, squinting at him. "A man. Saw him for a second. Then everything went black."

The same intruder? "Do you remember anything about him?"

"No. Something woke me up. I walked outside and got whacked upside the head."

"What time was that?" Trey mentally established a timeline.

"Not long after I'd gone to bed."

Trey helped Will to his feet, and they walked to the porch swing. Justine grabbed bottles of water from the fridge.

"We should get you to a hospital. You need stitches," Justine said.

"I ain't going to no hospital. Slap a Band-Aid on it, and it'll be fine," Will groused.

"Sorry, man. She's right," Trey said.

Will shook his head. "Can't afford no more bills."

"Why didn't you tell me you were having money issues?" Justine asked.

Will's neck jerked up. "Who told you?"

Justine bit her lip and looked at Trey. He sucked in a breath. She'd said humility was a great trait, though he doubted Will would agree.

"After the last break-in, I installed cameras on Justine's house and the barn," Trey confessed.

"Did they catch the creep that did this to me?" Will asked. Then, as if a light bulb appeared over his head, Will's eyes narrowed.

Trey braced for the explosion.

"Wait a minute. You spied on me?"

"It's not like that," Justine interjected.

"I wasn't sure you were trustworthy, Will. I misjudged you, and I'm sorry," Trey said. "By the way, I owe you a new Stetson."

Will opened his mouth, then closed it again. After a few seconds, he said, "No idea what that means, but I can't fault you for wanting what's best for Justine and the boys. So, uh, you saw me, uh, talking to the boys?"

Trey grinned.

Will sighed. "They're good listeners, and they don't charge me to whine."

"Canine therapy is the best," Trey agreed, ruffling Magnum's fur.

"Yeah, I s'pose you get that. Fact is, I'm embarrassed."

Justine touched his shoulder. "Don't be."

Will shrugged. "May as well come clean. Truth is, I've taken every job possible, but there ain't enough hours in the day to get them all done. And I didn't want to leave you in a lurch."

"I'm truly sorry, Will. I should've told you about the cameras." Justine shook her head.

"It's on me," Trey said.

"Nah, this is your property. You got the right to have surveillance equipment, although if they didn't catch the guy, seems they weren't installed properly." Will flicked a glance at Trey.

He absorbed the hit. It was true. The three cameras should've caught something to help them identify the intruder. "He knew to avoid them."

"You think he scoped out the place first?" Will asked.

"Must've." Trey rubbed the back of his neck.

Will frowned. "Could've come around when I wasn't paying attention. That's on me."

"You've been a godsend to me, Will. I'm grateful for all that you've done. Whoever is out to stop this investigation has made it their personal mission to destroy me. I wouldn't blame you for running for the hills right now." Justine glanced down.

"I don't run from nothin' and no one," Will asserted.

"Your insurance should cover the repairs," Trey said. The reply was weak and offered no real solution.

"Let's hope," Justine agreed. "But Will can't wait on a settlement's slow progress. I've got a little savings. We can use whatever's there to get started."

"Nathan Yancy owes me. I'll drag his young self out here to help," Will said.

Trey nodded. "With us in your corner, we'll figure something out. One day at a time."

"Can't take 'em no other way." Will snorted.

Trey chuckled and offered Will a handshake. "So, you're in?"

"You ain't seen nothin' yet. This old dog's still got some fight in him."

ELEVEN

Justine's breath hitched in her throat at the long rows of headstones and the spattering of color where loved ones' flowers spoke of their losses.

"You okay?" Trey asked, parking the truck.

"Yes."

"Will and Slade have things under control at the ranch. We have bigger fish to bake."

"Fry," Justine corrected.

Trey laughed. "Oliver's colloquialisms are wearing off on me."

Susan and Fredrick stood beside the large tractor prepared to tear into the ground.

"Nice to see their out-of-state trip allowed them to return in time for this," Trey said.

After asking for Susan to be brought in for questioning, Trey and Justine learned the Nolans had called Sergeant Oliver to notify him they'd be coming straight from the airport, having been out of town for a fundraising event. Their social media pictures provided proof of their airtight alibis for the night of the fire.

The walk to the grave was somber, and they stood at a distance, watching as the tractor's jaws removed layers of dirt, revealing the casket beneath. The worker hoisted the box from the ground and placed it on the trailer.

Trey and Justine returned to his pickup and drove

to the Omaha hospital where Taya McGill-Stryker prepped for the exam.

Entering the area just outside the pathology lab, Justine rushed to hug her friend. "Taya, thank you so much for coming."

They exchanged pleasantries and Taya said, "The remains should be ready. There was a little delay in getting them here. Something about car trouble. However, you won't be allowed in the lab. You can watch through the glass though." She disappeared through the swinging doors.

Justine and Trey moved to the lab viewing-room window. A steel table and a rectangular tool tray sat beside the casket. Taya entered, and the assistant lifted the lid.

A long pause.

"What's going on?" Trey whispered.

"I don't know."

Taya shook her head. She removed her gloves and exited the lab. Within a few seconds, she walked over to Trey and Justine. "We have a problem. There's no body."

"What?" Trey and Justine chimed in unison.

"The casket's empty."

"How's that possible? We were there when it was dug up," Trey insisted.

Taya lifted her hands. "All I can tell you is it's empty now."

"Was it left alone at any time?" Trey pressed.

"Only with the driver." Taya paused, then scurried out of the room.

Trey and Justine followed her to the loading area. The driver and truck were gone.

"Guess that explains the delay in the delivery." Taya shook her head.

Trey slammed his hands on the wall. "Unbelievable!"

Justine slumped onto a hard plastic chair. Her cell rang, interrupting the conversation, and she glanced at the screen before hitting Ignore.

"The Nolans got to the casket and stole the body," Trey said.

Justine's phone rang again with the same number. "Excuse me." She hurried from the loading dock, answering the call. "Justine Stark."

"Miss Stark, this is Mr. Krendal. I'm sorry to bother you during your time of mourning, but I'm the funeral director at Dearly Departed in Omaha, and your name is listed as the guarantor for the Grammert funeral."

"I beg your pardon?"

"Mrs. Victoria Grammert advised you'd be responsible for the bill. I'm sorry, but I must insist on payment before the services today, or we will not be able to fulfill our commitment."

Justine sucked in a breath. "What are you talking about? Ignaseus Grammert is dead?"

"Yes, ma'am, and the services are this afternoon at four o'clock. Without payment—"

"Do you have a number for Mrs. Grammert?"

"Yes." Mr. Krendal rattled off the ten digits.

"Please give me a moment. I'll call you right back." Justine disconnected and dialed the number.

"Hello." Victoria's quivering voice carried through the line.

"Mother, this is Justine. I just spoke with Mr. Krendal."

"Don't worry—I didn't tell him the great Justine Stark, criminal psychologist, was related to the lowly convict Ignaseus Grammert. I simply listed you as the guarantor of the services. A good daughter who would pay for her daddy's funeral."

How did her mother have the power to use Justine's achievements as swords to attack her with? Trey exited the loading dock and paused.

Justine shook her head and held up a hand, signaling him to stay back. "When did he die?"

"Why do you care? You wrote us off for that hag, Mrs. Scranton. But the least you can do is pay for your father's burial. You won't even have to leave the comfort of your home to do that."

The words were tiny daggers to Justine's heart. "When did he pass?" she asked again.

Trey moved closer, but Justine couldn't look at him. Yet she didn't walk away.

A part of her needed his comforting presence.

"Last week." Victoria sniffled.

Always the actress.

"So? Are you going to do the respectful thing? It's a daughter's duty."

Guilt swarmed Justine. She strove to behave honorably in everything. Did she owe it to her parents to absorb the costs? For once, maybe her mother had a point. Justine swallowed hard. "Yes. I'll handle the payment."

"Good." Victoria disconnected.

Justine pocketed her phone, her gaze fixed on the small octagon floor tiles. Her father was gone.

"Justine?" Trey slid beside her. "Are you okay?"

She turned as the ground gave out beneath her. Trey caught her in an embrace. Justine clung to him, allowing the tears to fall freely.

They stood that way until Justine could speak again.

"What happened? Who died?" Trey spoke softly, caressing her hair.

"My father." The words were so foreign. She backed away and dug out a tissue.

"Oh, I'm so sorry. Do you want to talk about it?"

She withdrew her phone. "Give me a few minutes alone, please. I need to call Mr. Krendal."

The need to be in control had Justine shifting into professionalism.

Trey nodded, then shoved his hands into his pockets and exited the room.

Justine secured the total amount for the funeral and agreed to meet Mr. Krendal at the home an hour before the services. She'd pay her respects without the other attendees seeing her and slip out before her mother arrived.

But the cost would drain a huge part of her savings account. What would she do about the ranch? How would she cover Will's labor and the supplies? Her head ached with the overwhelming questions stacking in a towering pile.

Trey returned with a cup of coffee for her. "I talked with Taya and she agreed to stick around. We're not letting the Nolans get away with this. I spoke to the hospital security manager and got footage of the driver, Pete Lucas, from their cameras. Sergeant Oliver is sending Eric the Vulture to bring Pete in for questioning."

"Good." Justine swallowed the lump in her throat. "Mind if we take a walk?"

"Sure. Let's get Magnum too."

With Magnum leashed, they strolled to a nearby park.

"I hate to ask this, but I need a ride to the funeral home later today."

"Of course. Whatever you require."

Justine smiled. "Somehow, I don't doubt you mean that, but you have no idea how much I could ask right now."

Trey stopped and faced her. "I'd do anything for you. I know that's corny, but it's true."

She shook her head. "Not if you really knew me."

Trey took her hand, enveloping it with his own. "Try me."

The need to unburden herself with why her father's death hurt but not like it would for a normal daughter propelled Justine forward.

They walked to a stone bench and sat.

"Sure you want to hear this?"

"Absolutely." Trey petted Magnum. "You have our undivided attention."

She chuckled. "Well, until he spots a squirrel or something."

Trey laughed. "Fair enough."

"My father's name is Ignaseus Grammert. My mother is Victoria. I changed my last name when I was eighteen and took my maternal grandmother's surname. I divorced myself from my parents."

Trey didn't speak and she continued, "You're probably thinking what an ungrateful brat I am."

"Actually, I'm wondering what pain caused you to make that drastic change."

She bit her quivering lip. His compassion squeezed her heart. "My father was physically abusive. Always angry. My mother sided with him. No matter what. Our home put the *fun* in *dysfunction*."

He chuckled. "Sorry."

She smiled. "No, I have to joke or I'll cry again."

He nodded. "I understand. Family relationships are the toughest. The old adage 'hurting people hurt people' applies here, because your parents both lived out of their pain. That's not an excuse."

"Yes. And I agree with the statement. I don't think anyone wakes up one morning determined to destroy another person's life. Even in murder cases I've worked, the act itself was rarely premeditated. More like an emotional volcano that burst."

"Attending your father's funeral would be closure for you."

He didn't understand. She removed her button-up shirt, revealing the matching tank top beneath it, and showed him the burn scars covering her arms. "That night, my father beat me senseless. For the first time, my mother tried to protect me, and he went after her too. We were unconscious when he covered the room in gasoline and lit the house on fire. Our next-door neighbor, a widow named Mrs. Scranton, heard the fire alarms going off and saw the flames." Justine's throat tightened. "She pulled us both from the blaze. One of those things where a person gets crazy strong and overcomes natural odds by sheer adrenaline. Anyway, she saved our lives. But my mother defended my father's actions and stood by him, even after he was convicted."

Trey's mouth hung open. "I don't know what to say."

Justine donned her shirt again, covering the scars. "I forgave them both years ago. At least, I started the process of forgiveness. Days like today, I feel as though I haven't made much progress. My mother signed my name guaranteeing the payment for my father's funeral."

"If you want to go, I'll be right beside you. If you decide it's too much to deal with, I'll support you.

Whatever you need, I'm here for you." The sincerity in Trey's eyes consumed Justine.

She looked down, and Trey took her hands in his, grounding her. "Why are you so good to me?"

"Because you're the most beautiful woman I've ever known. Inside and out."

Captured by his words, Justine was flooded with unfamiliar emotions.

Their gazes held while the rest of the world faded away.

Justine surrendered to her heart's cry, feathering her lips against Trey's. Their kiss was tender, tentative and full of promise.

Trey paced outside the interrogation-room door, his patience waning.

"You're making me nervous," Justine whispered.

"We know Pete's involved in the theft of Kayla's remains. Why is he lawyering up?"

Footsteps at the end of the hallway halted Trey's words. Alex Duncan approached. "I'll be Mr. Lucas's legal representative."

Trey glanced at Justine. "I should be astonished you're representing Lucas, but my surprise-meter is flat pegged out."

Alex held his briefcase with both hands, a smirk playing at the corners of his lips. "I will need a moment to confer with my client."

"Have at it." Trey gestured toward the room.

Justine blocked the entry and shifted out of the

way, allowing Alex to enter. He closed the door softly behind him.

"This is ridiculous. Why can't we just haul in the Nolans?" Justine's question was more comment than inquiry.

Trey resumed pacing the hallway until Alex peered out.

"We're ready," he announced.

Justine entered first, and they moved to the chairs across the table from Pete and Alex.

Pete's knee bounced, and he bit a fingernail with nervous vigor.

Guilty. "I'm curious why you're his lawyer," Trey said.

"Pete's worked for the Nolans in the past, and they wanted to help him," Alex said dryly.

Trey snorted. "Now that your *attorney* is here, tell me where Kayla Nolan's remains are."

Alex's blank facial expression matched his monotone response. "My client is only responsible for exhuming the casket, which you both witnessed. He provided that service appropriately and efficiently."

"Right up to the point where he detoured and the contents mysteriously disappeared," Trey snapped.

Pete opened his mouth, but Alex shook his head. "The contents aren't his responsibility."

"They are when he either organized or performed the theft," Trey said.

Pete leaned forward, a bead of sweat easing down his brow. "I only did what I was—"

"Don't say another word or I cannot help you," Alex instructed.

Pete slunk down in the seat and resumed fingernail biting and knee bouncing.

"We have security-camera footage showing Pete pulling up at the hospital twenty minutes after the expected arrival time. That gives him plenty of opportunity to drop off the remains somewhere else. I will recommend charging your client with obstruction of justice, among other things." Trey stood.

Pete jumped up. "No!" He addressed Alex. "You said—"

Alex placed a hand on the young man's shoulder, pulling him down. "I said we would handle this." Then to Trey, "My client may have information on the body's location, but before we say anything, I want the assurance that he will not be implicated in any way."

Justine jerked to look at Trey, desperation in her expression. "We need the remains."

As if that were news, but Trey agreed. Charging Lucas would only delay the exhumation. Still, allowing him to go unpunished somehow rewarded the Nolans. Trey leaned back and crossed his arms. "If I get information—solid, verifiable details—and the remains are recovered in their entirety, I will not recommend charges against him."

Alex slapped both hands on the table and Pete startled in his chair. "Very good. We'll be in touch." Alex stood. "Let's get you out of here."

Trepidation hung in Pete's eyes, but he willingly followed Alex from the room.

Justine rose and peered out the door, then closed it. "What if he doesn't provide anything?"

"He will."

Ten minutes later, a text message rang through with GPS coordinates from an unknown number. "Chicken," Trey mumbled.

"He sent the information?" Justine looked over his shoulder.

"Possibly. It came from a blocked number. I'll ask Sergeant Oliver to handle it from here. You and I need to leave for the funeral."

Justine glanced down. "Yeah, I guess so."

Oliver answered on the first ring. "Well?"

"Alex Duncan's representing Lucas," Trey began.

Oliver mumbled something unpleasant. "Did he give you anything?"

"Yeah, as long as we don't charge Lucas. I had to agree to it, boss. We need the remains."

"That should've been my decision, but I'd have done the same. And?"

"I'll text you the message with the location that Alex sent over." Trey concluded the call with the request to have Oliver accompany Taya.

"Consider it handled. I'll stay with her through the examination, as well. Please give Justine our condolences."

"Will do. Thanks, boss."

"Everything okay?" Justine asked.

"Yep." Trey offered his most encouraging smile, and they walked out to the truck.

The funeral home wasn't far from the patrol office, and a few cars filled the parking lot. They'd arrived early enough to avoid the mourners.

Trey and Magnum accompanied Justine to the business office, where she paid the bill. He stood outside the door, but his cop instincts took over and he listened in. When Krendal announced the amount due, Trey sucked in a breath. Her mother had apparently spared no expense since Justine was responsible. A slow simmer of anger welled inside him.

Justine made no qualms about it but silently handed over her credit card. Trey wondered how the drain on her finances would affect the repairs to the ranch. As much as he wanted to rush in and settle the bill for her, Trey knew it wasn't his place.

"Mr. Krendal, would it be possible for me to pay my respects before the visitation?" Justine asked.

"Absolutely."

She exited the office with a blank expression. Her gait was stiff, almost robotic, as Krendal led them to the viewing. Soft music played, and an open casket stood at the front of the room.

"Take your time." Krendal closed the doors behind them.

"Would you like me to go with you?" Trey asked.

Justine shook her head.

He waited with Magnum at the last row.

She didn't move for several beats. Then, in painfully slow steps, she approached the casket. Trey's heart squeezed, desperate to help her and completely clueless how to do that.

She'd nearly reached the casket when a slender woman with strikingly similar features to Justine's entered from a side door. "You've got a lot of nerve. Don't touch him."

"Hello, Mother." Justine's voice was steely, but Trey recognized the vulnerability beneath the tough exterior.

He stepped forward. This was Victoria Grammert? "Excuse me."

Victoria's lip curled. "This is *my* husband's funeral. I have the right to say who can and cannot be here, Officer." She practically spit the last word. "Did you handle the bill?"

"Yes," Justine answered.

Satisfaction covered Victoria's face. "Good. Then you're free to go." She waved them off. "Don't waste your time pretending you care about me or your father."

Justine held her chin high. "I'd like to pay my respects."

"Why? I haven't had a daughter for twenty years. You're a stranger, and strangers aren't welcome here."

People began filing into the room.

Justine stood frozen just a few feet from the coffin. Trey moved to her side. "Let's go."

Victoria stepped forward, blocking Justine. "Get out! You're too good for us. Always have been. You turned your back on us. You kept him behind those prison walls! You stopped him from having a real life, just to hang on to your bitterness." Victoria's voice rose with each word.

Trey put an arm around Justine's waist. "Come on. Let's go."

She nodded, shuffling beside him. A woman ran to the front to comfort the now-wailing Victoria, and the other mourners looked on with curiosity.

The trip to the truck was excruciating.

"I'm so sorry, Justine."

She released a bitter laugh. "I walked into that."

"You did the right thing, and you did not deserve that attack."

"Maybe I did." Justine glanced down, one hand rubbing her arm.

"Don't let Victoria do that to you. She's angry and hurting. I'm sure she didn't mean those awful things." Trey hoped that was true, but something told him Victoria intended the cruelty and the show.

"Oh, she did." Justine looked up, tears welling in her eyes.

Trey reached for her, and she crumbled into his arms, her body racked with sobs.

He shouldn't have encouraged Justine to attend the funeral. Seeing her hurt was agonizing, and he longed to take away her pain. *Lord, I need wisdom here.*

He turned so Justine's back faced the people filing into the building. Several glanced at them. Did they know Justine was Ignaseus's daughter? A few pointed and shook their heads.

He held Justine tighter, anxious to guard her from their judgmental faces. And in that moment, Trey realized he needed Justine in a way he'd never needed anyone before.

She was much more than a colleague. He cared what happened to her. He wanted her to be happy. He wanted to protect her.

He wanted to be a part of her life.

But what if she didn't feel the same way? She'd established defined boundaries of their relationship.

Yet they'd shared a kiss. One that had rocked him to his core, igniting a place in his heart reserved for only Justine.

Trey's cell phone rang, dragging him to the present, but he didn't move.

Justine leaned back. "Answer it. I'm okay."

"It's Oliver," Trey said, glancing at the screen. "Sir."

"The body has been secured. Dr. McGill-Stryker will begin her examination immediately."

Trey exhaled relief. Finally, some good news. "Outstanding."

"Jackson, you should know the Nolans have gone to the colonel."

"With what?"

Oliver sighed. "They're accusing you and Miss

Stark of an inappropriate relationship, claiming it's interfering with the case and the profile."

"That's ridiculous!" Trey paced an area beside his truck, feeling Justine's eyes on him.

Were the Nolans following them?

"I'm a realist, Jackson, and it wouldn't be the first time romance invaded a case," Oliver said, referring to Trey's brother, Slade, who'd fallen for a murder suspect.

"That's not what's happening here. Miss Stark and I are purely professional and platonic. Neither of us has any romantic interest in the other."

Justine faced him, hurt in her eyes.

"See that you keep it professional. Otherwise, I'll have to take you off the case."

"Understood." Trey disconnected.

Justine folded her arms, donning her clinical exterior. "Now what?"

He reluctantly gave her an abbreviated version of the discussion.

"Of course there's nothing going on between us. We shared a kiss—that never should've happened—but surely they didn't see that? Even if they did, it meant nothing." Justine's tone hardened.

"Are you upset with me?"

"No. We're partnered on a case. I appreciate the kindness you offered for my father's funeral. It won't be needed again." Justine gripped the truck door handle. "Let's get moving."

Trey loaded Magnum and slid behind the wheel.

Justine sat erect in the seat, face set like flint.

"There's good news. Kayla's remains have been recovered, and Dr. McGill-Stryker will start the exam immediately."

Justine nodded. "Great."

"You've had an awful day. Let's head back to the ranch so you can rest."

"No, we have to keep working. I need the distraction, and if the Nolans are as unreliable about the seventy-two hours as they have been about everything else, we can't risk running out of time. We have the case files—or what's left of them after the water damage—with us. Let's find a place to go through them."

"We can return to the patrol office so that we're close to where Dr. McGill-Stryker is working."

"Perfect."

The drive was too quiet, but Trey was at a loss for words.

Once seated in the room, they spread out the files.

An insurance document caught Trey's eye. "The Nolans had a life insurance policy on Kayla."

"How much?"

"Seven hundred thousand." He scanned the document. "It was paid out to them—" he pointed to the case file "—just prior to Drazin's retirement date."

"The amount is odd. Not a million or half a million?" Justine asked.

"An off amount would deflect from suspicion?"

"But why? They're not in dire straits. Who's the beneficiary?"

"They are."

"They could've hired someone to kill Kayla or…" Justine hesitated, a pen pressed against her lips. "You said it was paid out before Drazin retired. What if he was the recipient?"

"It should be easy enough to trace." But Sergeant Oliver's warning rang in Trey's mind. He couldn't accuse Drazin of taking a bribe, and as much as he didn't like the guy, he didn't believe he'd murdered Kayla. "We need the Nolans' financial records."

Trey typed an email to Sergeant Oliver, making the formal request.

"May I look at the insurance policy?"

Trey passed her the document.

Justine's eyes widened. "Hmm, interesting. There's a Slayer Rule to the policy."

"You lost me."

"If the Nolans are found to be involved in Kayla's death, they'd have to repay the money. Let's park this for now until we can get a hold of their financial records." Justine's phone rang. "It's Alex Duncan."

"Put it on speaker."

"Hello, Alex," Justine said.

"Miss Stark. I need to talk to you."

"We're here at the patrol office."

"No. You and Trey must meet with me in person. Enough is enough. I have what you need, but if the Nolans discover I'm the one who gave it to you, I'm a dead man."

"Alex, why should we believe you?" Trey asked.

"You shouldn't, but I can tell you that without the evidence I have, you'll never solve the case. With it, you'll have everything you need for a conviction. So I guess you'll have to decide if it's worth it to you."

Justine met Trey's eyes. He gave a slight nod.

"Okay. Where?"

"I'll send you the address. Meet me there at ten o'clock tonight. I have one chance to right the wrong done to Kayla."

TWELVE

"Remind me why we're doing this." Justine walked the perimeter of the abandoned warehouse, her footsteps echoing. The dank smell of dust and mold filled the atmosphere.

"I'm asking myself the same question, but Alex has evidence. Maybe he grew a conscience or got tired of Susan's antics. Who knows? At least this time we're prepared with backup." Trey withdrew his gun and checked his magazine.

"I'm amazed you requested Eric Irwin's help." Justine peered through a corner of a spiderweb-covered window. She searched the parking lot, but Irwin was nowhere to be seen. Not that he would be, since he was hidden, watching the exterior.

A comfort and a concern.

"Okay, let's not confuse technicalities. I didn't request Irwin. I requested backup and Oliver offered Irwin. Big difference," Trey clarified.

She chuckled. "Duly noted. It's progress for your relationship."

"Doubtful." His cell phone buzzed, and he placed the call on speaker. "We're in position."

"Same here," Eric replied. "No one has gone in or out. Sure you don't want Apollo to do recon?"

Trey rolled his eyes and Justine stifled a giggle. "No, we've got it, but if you see anything—"

"We'll come to your rescue," Eric concluded.

Trey visibly bristled. "Or just cover us."

"Roger that."

Pocketing his phone, Trey said, "He's nothing if not enthusiastic. There's still time, if you'd rather stay with Irwin. Magnum and I can handle Alex and you'd be at a safer distance."

"No way." They'd had this conversation ten ways from Sunday already.

"Stay here. I want to do one more run-through."

Justine hopped up onto a cement dock space and watched as Trey and Magnum moved through the small warehouse, clearing it with expertise and precision. An office near the back was void, except for a file cabinet, and the rest of the building was a large open area. A few pallets littered the floor. Otherwise, it too was empty.

Trey returned to her side. "He's running late."

"What's the evidence Alex is holding?"

"I don't know, but it better be good."

Magnum sat panting at Trey's feet, clad in his camouflage-patterned, patrol–K-9 vest.

"Poor guy. It's hot in here. I can't imagine wearing fur and a vest," Justine said, petting the sweet dog.

"The vest gives me a way to carry him in an emergency, and it's bulletproof."

Justine straightened. "In that case, keep it on him. He seems to be moving better, not favoring one side as much."

"I noticed that too." Trey glanced at his watch. "Alex's got five minutes, and we're out of here."

Justine reached into her pocket and withdrew the diary. "Can I borrow your flashlight?"

"How about teamwork? I'll hold. You read."

"Works for me." Justine inspected the book, careful to separate the pages. "It's dry and most of the pages are legible." She flipped to the end and pressed the journal flat on her thighs. "Oh, there's a little damage to the back cover." A corner of the last page was lifted. "Hey, move that light here."

Trey did as she asked, and Justine gently wedged her fingers beneath the crinkled paper. "It looks like these extra pages were glued down on purpose."

"Why do that?"

Justine further separated them, revealing a small silver key. "What do we have here?" She pried the key from the tiny pocket and passed it to Trey.

"It's too small to open a door. A lockbox? Or a padlock?" He handed it back, and she turned it over in her hand.

"I don't know. But it's obviously important." Justine peeled the paper back even more. "And she wrote *Underwood Machler* beside it."

"A name? Location?"

Justine shrugged.

"Did she write anything about the key in the diary?" Trey asked.

"I don't think so. I didn't memorize the book, but

I don't remember anything that said 'by the way, I hid a key that has whatever in it,'" she teased.

"Funny."

Justine slipped the key into the diary and dropped it into her pants pocket. They hadn't talked about the Nolans' accusation or Trey's emphatic denial of a romantic relationship. Logic told her there was nothing wrong with what he'd said, but her pride stung. The shared kiss was an impulsive, emotional action. Nevertheless, she'd enjoyed it and imagined he had too. Still, she wouldn't jeopardize his career over a kiss, especially because the Nolans fought dirty.

"I never said thank-you for what you did at the funeral. I'm sorry the Nolans have the impression we're engaged in inappropriate behavior."

Trey winced. "I hope I didn't offend you by what I said to Sergeant Oliver."

"No. I totally get it. We're coworkers."

Hurt flashed in Trey's eyes, but he nodded. "Exactly. Nothing more."

"That kiss never should've happened. It was a fluke. I didn't read anything more into it. In case you were wondering." She was rambling and justifying. He'd see right through her.

"Just a flurry of emotion." Trey glanced at his watch. "And we're done. Alex isn't coming. This is a joke." His cell phone buzzed. "Yeah, I said the same thing. Sorry for wasting your time. We were played. Nah, go ahead and leave. We're doing the same." Trey pocketed his phone. "Let's get out of here."

Disappointment weighed down Justine's shoulders. "I thought we'd get a break in the case."

"There's got to be a clue in the diary about the key, and now we know to look for it."

They slid off the cement dock step and walked to the door. Trey gripped the handle. "It's locked." He thrust his shoulder against it, but the door didn't budge.

"Must've locked behind us." Justine turned. An exit sign glowed from the other side of the warehouse. "There's another door. We can go out that way."

They crossed the space and pushed it open without issue. She paused and peered outside. They were on the opposite side of the building, near a retaining wall with overgrown weeds.

"All clear." Justine stepped out first, her foot brushing something.

Magnum barked and took off running up the sloped ground. He disappeared into the vegetation.

In what felt like slow motion, she turned to Trey.

He lifted her and lunged away from the building.

A blast propelled them into the air, exploding the space with a vicious orange light.

They landed hard on the pavement, and Trey covered her, pressing down on Justine as metal and wood showered them.

She tried not to breathe in the dirt, and her

body didn't move for what felt like hours. Her ears rang with a deafening sound so intense her brain throbbed.

Trey shifted, helping Justine to her feet. His lips moved, but she couldn't hear him. He put his hands around his mouth, calling in the direction the dog had run off to. Then he hopped onto the retaining wall and sprinted into the weeds. Justine's legs were heavy and her body ached, but she followed, stepping up to the higher ground. Where had Trey gone?

"Magnum!" Trey's voice broke through the ringing in her ears. The sound distant but strong. A flashlight swept across an area to her right.

Justine jogged to him. His cries for Magnum were growing more desperate and frequent. Worry etched Trey's face, along with several scrapes and cuts from the blast.

The warehouse continued to smolder below.

Together, they searched the grasslands, taking turns calling his name. The property merged into a large field leading to the highway.

Headlights illuminated the roadway below.

Lord, help us!

Where had Magnum gone? Was he hurt?

In the distance, movement in her peripheral vision caught Justine's attention. She spun and spotted Magnum running. No, he was limping.

Oh, please be okay. Justine took off, and Trey joined her, closing the gap to where Magnum approached, half running, half limping.

Trey lifted him, holding the animal against his heaving chest and burying his face in Magnum's neck.

Justine looked up, scanning the area. "I don't see anyone out there."

Trey shifted Magnum to her arms. "Stay here." He hurried off in the direction from where Magnum had run to them, then returned within a few minutes. "Whatever or whoever he was chasing is long gone."

Justine inspected his paws, and Magnum jerked when she touched his previously injured paw. "He's hurt."

"Let's get back to the truck." Trey took Magnum and cradled him as they traipsed to the warehouse.

Eric's patrol truck sat in the parking lot. He and Apollo approached. "I saw the explosion when I reached the main road and turned around. Already got fire rescue on the way."

Emphasizing his words, sirens screamed in the distance.

"Convenient you were gone when the blast happened," Trey shot.

Justine gaped at him. "Trey—"

"What're you saying?" Eric stood taller.

Trey brushed past him. "Read it how you want. You were supposed to be our backup."

"And you told me to go," Eric argued.

"Yeah, and how was it someone just happened to get an IED trip wire set up in the only exit available and you never saw it happening?" Trey's voice grew louder, and he still cradled Magnum.

"Gentlemen!" Justine stepped between them. "This isn't the time or the place." She faced Trey. "Take care of Magnum."

"He's hurt?" Eric moved beside them, genuine concern written in his eyes.

"Right before the blast, Magnum went after someone, but we never saw who. He must've lost him," Justine explained.

Eric nodded. "I'll take Apollo through there and see if he can get a scent."

Trey and Justine walked to his patrol truck, and Trey worked to inspect Magnum's wound. "Thank you for interrupting back there. We probably would've thrown fists."

"You're upset. Understandably, but at the wrong person."

"Irwin should've seen someone if they set that IED wire."

"Unless it'd been rigged before we got here."

"I have a friend at the ATF. I'll ask him to investigate." Worry creased Trey's forehead. "Mags, are you okay? I'm not sure what happened." The sadness in his eyes tore at Justine.

"He could've stepped on something. A sticker?"

Trey shook his head. "No. It's worse than that. If he reinjured the wound, Magnum may not be able to work anymore." He stroked the animal's neck.

"You were right. I should've left him behind at the ranch. What if he's permanently injured?"

"Let's not throw the dog out with the bathwater."

"Now you sound like Oliver." Trey's smile didn't reach his eyes.

"Have his veterinarian check him over before you make any rash decisions."

Trey spun to face her. "Justine, you've seen him. He wants to work, but unless he's out of commission for a lengthy time, I'm not sure he'll ever get back to his normal self." He looked past her where Eric and Apollo were working the hillside. "Maybe it's time for him to retire."

Justine remained silent, unsure what to say.

Trey reached for his radio. "Possible bombing. BOLO for suspect Alex Duncan, believed to be involved," he continued, responding to the dispatcher's request for specifics.

Justine stroked Magnum's ears. *Lord, is all of this hopeless? Please help Magnum.*

Would the key provide any clue?

Trey returned to her. "When I get my hands on Alex—" He slammed his hand on the truck, pacing in front of her. "He lured us here, had that trip wire placed where we wouldn't see it. Even had the door locked behind us."

"You'll get him," Justine assured him.

He sighed, scrubbing his head. "Okay. I'm better." Trey gently removed Magnum's vest. "You did good, buddy." He stepped back, closing the door, and paused. "Hey, what's this?"

Justine leaned in, and he withdrew a flashlight, aiming it at the smear.

"I think it's blood, but I need an ALS to confirm."

"Alternative light source?" she clarified.

"Yes. If I'm right, the ALS will cause the blood to glow blue. Then we'll ask the lab to take a sample. Magnum must've gotten a hold of the perp!" Hope danced in his eyes.

"I don't mean to be a downer, but wouldn't we need a known sample to run the blood against?"

"One step at a time. Stay optimistic. We'll catch whoever did this."

"Magnum didn't just injure his paw. It's possible the perp hit or kicked him."

Trey's jaw tightened. "Definitely. Let's go to the troop office. They'll have an ALS."

"But will the lab run the sample now?"

"No, but with a little begging, maybe they'll do it first thing in the morning."

THIRTEEN

Dr. Taya McGill-Stryker's announcement worked to drain the color from Fredrick Nolan's face. Like a week-old helium balloon, the man shriveled before Justine. She stifled a yawn, the aftermath of a busy evening and talking late into the night with Taya. There'd been no time to return to the ranch, so Justine had bunked in Taya's hotel room while Trey had lodged with a friend. They'd met with the lab after confirming the smear on Magnum's vest was indeed blood. And the day was flying by.

"Are you absolutely certain?" Fredrick's voice cracked with age and shock, dragging Justine to the present.

Susan Nolan's eyes widened, and her cheeks reddened. "You're making that up. Trying to justify the intrusion and desecration of Kayla's grave site."

"I assure you that is not the goal. I am an independent forensic anthropologist brought in to perform the evaluation without bias. My findings are documented and absolute. You may view the report for yourself," Taya said.

"Oh, believe me, we will," Susan bit out.

"Where? How?" Fredrick flattened his hands on the table, as if holding on for dear life.

"I discovered a fragmented tip of a needle embedded in Kayla's spine," Taya explained for the second time.

"But that doesn't prove anything," Susan argued.

"Actually, the location confirms Kayla did not voluntarily overdose. I found traces of the narcotics in her spine, as well. The trajectory makes it physically impossible for Kayla to have injected herself. I'm marking her file as a murder," Taya said.

Fredrick's shoulders slumped, and he covered his face. "My beautiful Kayla. What have we done?"

The strange comment grabbed Justine's attention, and based on the expressions of the others present at the interrogation table, she wasn't the only one.

The shift in Fredrick's pain touched Justine. "Mr. Nolan, with this information, I believe it's a reasonable assumption someone staged your daughter's murder to look like an overdose. But who wanted her dead? Is there anything you remember that might help us?"

"This is ridiculous," Susan argued. "Nothing has changed, from our point of view. Kayla's death was a tragedy, but after all this time, what difference will changing the cause of it make?"

Justine gaped at the woman. "For one, we need to get a murderer off the streets."

"Unless you've found evidence, how will that happen?" Susan shot back.

Fredrick rejoined the conversation, tears pooling in his eyes. "Kayla wasn't using drugs?"

Taya shook her head. "I wish I could answer that to your satisfaction, but there's not enough evidence one way or the other."

"She wasn't," Justine defended her friend.

"I wanted to protect her." Fredrick folded his hands on the table. "It was my doing. I asked Pete Lucas to steal Kayla's body."

"Fredrick!" Susan said. "Don't say another word."

"It's time we told them." He addressed Justine. "After talking with you, Susan and I had a long discussion and she convinced me Kayla's reputation would be dragged through the mud along with ours. The media outlets were relentless the first time. I wanted to protect my family."

Susan's hand flew to her neck, where a large solitaire diamond hung from a thick rope chain. "You're blaming me?"

"No, I'm stating the facts." He sat back.

"Mr. Nolan, do you realize what you're saying?" Trey intervened.

Fredrick nodded.

"You'll be charged with tampering with the body," Trey added.

"I understand and accept full responsibility. Whatever you need from me, I promise my cooperation."

"I'll try to keep your charges to a minimum," Trey promised.

"Thank you."

"Mr. Nolan, I found something in Kayla's diary and wondered if you'd be willing to help me," Justine inquired.

"Yes, of course."

"Does the name Underwood Machler mean anything to you?" Justine asked.

He started to shake his head. "No, I—"

Susan jumped to her feet. "This is preposterous! My husband is obviously not feeling well and speaking from grief. Which you are taking advantage of. We're leaving. If you need something, contact Alex Duncan."

Trey stood. "We'd love to. The BOLO issued for him is still active. Any idea where he is?"

Susan's lips narrowed into a thin line. She gripped Fredrick's arm and hauled him up, then dragged him from the room, slamming the door behind her.

"Wow," Taya said, facing Justine.

"Thank you again for everything."

"I'm grateful I could help. Kayla deserves justice. I'll be praying for you both. I'll finish my investigation notes and get my finding to Sergeant Oliver today before I leave." Taya gathered her files, and after a hug with Justine and a handshake with Trey, she exited the room.

"Is it me or did Susan seem to go off the deep end at the mention of Underwood Machler?" Justine asked.

"Um, yeah. Not sure if it was the name or the fact her husband confessed to stealing the body," Trey said.

Justine's phone rang. A glance at the screen sent her stomach into knots. Everything within her wanted to ignore the call, but experience had long ago taught her Victoria wouldn't give up. "Hello."

"Justine. Oh, honey, I'm so sorry for how I behaved yesterday." Victoria's words dripped with sweetness.

Typical. Attack. Apologize. Repeat. Justine sucked in a breath. "You're grieving."

"I am, darling, but that's no excuse. Forgive me. After you'd gone, it hit me I'm all alone. And I can't bear that." Based on the sniffles and hiccups, Victoria was crying.

How many times had Justine heard her mother speak those words as justification after Ignaseus's angry beatings? Yet a trickle of hope from her traitorous heart clung to one word. *Family.* Hadn't Trey told her it was time to forgive her parents? Was this the step in doing that? "I forgive you."

Victoria sniffled. "Thank you. Honey, I'll be returning to North Platte—that's where I live."

Justine refrained from saying "I know." Though they hadn't spoken, she'd kept tabs on her parents. "I'm glad you called before you left."

"Thing is, I had to talk with you today."

Justine braced herself. Of course Victoria would call with ulterior motives.

"I did my best to be a good wife and mother. Even after that nasty Mrs. Scranton stole you away from me."

Justine gripped the table with her free hand. Her mother always put down Mrs. Scranton, but the woman had saved Justine's life. Figuratively and literally.

Victoria continued, "We all made sacrifices, and as much as your desertion devastated your father and I, I forgive you too."

Warning signs blared. Victoria was warming up for the kill.

"You're successful and can afford the funeral-service bill. I have nothing. Not even enough to bury the love of my life. The ceremony was beautiful. It's too bad you weren't able to stay."

Justine bit her lip to stop the retort dying to escape, and redirected the conversation. "I wish I'd known sooner."

Victoria sighed. "I'm sorry. But I need a little help to get me by. You see, I lost my job when your father fell ill, but I had to be by his side."

Always Ignaseus's defender, no matter the cost. "How much do you need?" Justine cut to the chase.

"I hate to ask, but ten thousand would be great."

Justine gasped. "I don't have that kind of money. I've recently endured some—" she considered what to tell her mother and opted for limited information "—damage to my house. I could probably swing a few hundred."

"That's just like you. So selfish. Take care of number one! Forget it, Justine. Stay out of my life." Victoria hung up.

Justine stared at the phone, disbelieving.

"I'm scared to ask," Trey said.

The comfort of her clinician persona provided a shield, and Justine slotted Victoria into the role of patient. "Apparently the amount I offered wasn't good enough. I won't hear from her again." She glanced down at her hands. What must Trey Jackson, with the perfect family, think of her pathetic one's brokenness?

"I'm proud of you."

Her head jerked up. "What? You are?" Justine sighed. "I could take out a loan or something."

"Absolutely not."

She looked at him.

"Sorry, that's not my place, but, Justine, going into debt isn't the way to help her. Setting boundaries is healthy for both of you."

Logically, he was correct. Her training agreed. But guilt weighed on her heart. "What kind of daughter refuses her mother?"

"Had you heard from Victoria before today?"

"Not since I moved in with Mrs. Scranton my sophomore year of high school."

"Not once?"

"No."

Trey put an arm around her shoulder. "You did the right thing."

"Is it stupid that a part of me wants to give her the money, just to be accepted again?" She hated herself for admitting the embarrassing truth.

Trey took her hand. "Every child longs for their parent's approval."

"I want to be worth something to someone." The confession slipped out before she could stop it, and she longed to retrieve it.

Trey dropped to a squat beside her. "Your value isn't based on your mother's inaccurate view of love."

She rose, creating distance between them. "You don't understand. Your family is perfect, and you'll have one of your own someday. I'll always be broken, trying to be normal and never measuring up."

Trey laughed and stood.

Justine startled. "Nice. Laugh at me when I'm vulnerable."

"I'm sorry. I didn't mean to offend you. My family is far from perfect. There's just more of us to carry the chaos evenly."

She grinned. "Whatever."

"Seriously. We've got our own sets of problems and battles. If not for God's grace and a lot of prayer between us, we would've fallen apart many times." He sobered. "You make your own future. No matter what's happened, your parents' dysfunction is not a direct reflection on you. Anyone who knows you has seen you're brilliant, beautiful, compassionate, beautiful—"

"You already said *beautiful*."

"It's worth repeating." That delicious dimple of his reappeared. "We're all responsible for ourselves, accountable for our own actions. You've proved you're an amazing woman."

Justine averted her eyes, cheeks warm. But if Trey meant all those things, why had he adamantly denied they were involved when Sergeant Oliver called?

"Say it."

"What?"

"I smell smoke," he teased.

Justine grinned. "I don't mean to dispute your kind words, but if you think that, why did you tell Sergeant Oliver we weren't involved? Not that we are, but your emphatic rejection seemed over-the-top."

Trey's brows met in a triangle. "I apologize if I came off that way. I was so angry at the Nolans and thought about Susan's warning to you. I wanted to make sure they didn't have any ammunition to destroy our reputations and careers. If I were responsible for that kind of devastation, it'd kill me. I care for you. Too much."

He cared. For her. What did that mean? It didn't matter. They'd agreed romance wasn't a possibility. He was a nice guy. "Thank you. That makes me feel better." Changing topics, Justine pushed in the chairs. "We should get out of here. Poor Magnum needs an outdoor break." She gestured to where the dog lay dozing in the corner.

"Yeah, he looks pretty eager to move." Trey chuckled. "While we're clearing the air, I have to tell you something."

Justine's heart thudded against her ribs. "Okay."

"I'm sorry for not calling out Victoria at the funeral. Maybe that would've prevented her money attempt."

"Ever the optimist? Rest assured you handled the situation well. Victoria's a drama queen. She would've raised the roof worse than she did if you'd have stepped in."

Trey shrugged and perched on the end of the table. Clearly, he wasn't leaving the room anytime soon. Justine leaned against the wall.

"Failing to protect people I care about is the one thing I excel at. Always has been."

"What do you mean?"

Trey sighed. "Forget about it. I'm whining."

"I blurted my ugly history and confessions. Your turn. Whine away." Justine smiled.

He grinned. "I guess that's a fair trade." He slid onto a chair, and she did the same, keeping the table between them. "I love my job. Serving the public and working with Magnum is a dream come true for me. But I'm always chasing this ghost from my past."

"Does this ghost have a name?"

"There was a kid, Josh, a senior when I was a sophomore. He was fun, the class clown, football star, but he had major drinking issues. He was nice, and I was thrilled an upperclassman paid attention to me."

"Wasn't Slade already including you in his group?"

Trey shrugged. "It's different. I hated being in

Slade's shadow. Josh treated me as an equal, not like Slade's little brother. Ya know?"

She nodded, and he continued, "We were at a graduation party. Josh was there, being his usual corny self, but he disappeared for a while, so I searched for him. Found Josh by the pool, downing a large amount of alcohol. He was drunk, staggering around, and he headed for his pickup. I offered to drive him home. Josh was three times my size. I know it's hard to believe, looking at my athletic physique now, but I was really scrawny." Trey puffed out his chest like a rooster.

Justine laughed.

"Hey, it's not that funny."

"Sorry. Go on."

"Anyway, I tried to stop him. Took his keys and ran away. Not smart. Mr. Football Star tackled me. He lifted me by the shirt, threw a solid uppercut and tossed me into the pool."

The smile fell from Justine's face. "No."

"Yep, it was humiliating. Everyone laughed, and I slunk away to lick my wounds. Josh died that night in a drunk-driving accident."

Justine's hands flew to her mouth. "I'm so sorry."

"Shook me up for a while. Kept thinking I should've done something more to stop him. The same way I felt after Victoria unleashed on you at the funeral."

"Trey, you were a kid."

"That's no excuse. I should've called the cops or flattened his tires."

"Is that why you joined the patrol?"

"Yep. I wanted to protect people. But we see how well that's turning out."

Justine rounded the table and perched on the edge beside Trey. "No one controls another's destiny. You did what you could with what you had."

Trey didn't look up.

"Do you remember Nathan Yancy?"

That got his attention. "The kid who drove Will to your place."

"Yes. Can you imagine tagging him with the guilt of a classmate's death?"

"No."

"Exactly."

"But it's not just Josh. Kayla too. I should've done more. I spend so much of my life with *should've*, *could've*, *would've*. So what? I'm not helping anyone."

"You make a difference daily. I've never been in more danger than I have in the past few days, and you're always there. I'm grateful for your presence. But I understand reliving the pain of the past. I'll give you the advice I remind myself of. 'Absolve yourself for that night and receive God's forgiveness for any shortcomings you're clinging to. Because He's not holding them against you.'"

Trey smiled. "You're smart."

"I know, right? I have student loans to prove I paid to learn all that smartness." She grinned.

"Now, if only we'd get the results from the blood from Magnum's vest."

At the mention of his name, Magnum stretched and opened one eye.

A single knock preceded a trooper peering around the door. "This just came in." He handed the paper to Trey and disappeared.

Justine moved beside him. "Well?"

"It's the results of the blood test."

"And?"

"No known match."

Trey leaned back and closed his eyes, frustration oozing through his veins. They'd spent hours reviewing the case evidence with no leads. He glanced again at the lab test. "How's it possible to have blood—DNA proof—from the perp who set that IED and still have nothing?"

"All we need is a comparison sample."

"You make it sound so simple."

"Trying to stay optimistic," Justine said. "And we have the key." She smoothed the diary on the table and flipped to the back cover. "That wasn't visible before."

Trey leaned over, spotting a sticker depicting a stylized blue jay.

Justine's eyes widened.

"I smell smoke."

She jumped to her feet and glanced at her watch. "We have to hurry before they close."

"Where?"

"I'll tell you on the way." Justine shoved the case files into the box and hurried out of the room.

Trey leashed Magnum. "Sorry, buddy, the boss lady says we've got a lead."

His partner lazily opened an eye, peering from beneath his eyebrows, then slowly pushed to a sitting position. Guilt coursed through him. Magnum should stay behind at the patrol office. "Hey, Mags, sit this one out."

Magnum stood and gave a thorough shake from head to tail in an emphatic disapproval of the offer.

Trey grinned. Or not.

Justine was already down the hall by the time he and Magnum caught up with her.

"I love a good mystery, but since I'm driving, think you could clue me in to the details on this one?" he teased, loading Magnum into his kenneled area.

"Hurry!" Justine slid onto the passenger seat and closed the door.

Trey rushed to get behind the wheel.

A huge smile played on Justine's face and her hazel eyes sparkled. "Pierce."

Trey blinked and started the engine. "I'm going to need a little more information."

"The town of Pierce."

"Because—"

"If my suppositions are correct, we need to open a safe-deposit box from the First Bank of Pierce."

"And…" Trey headed toward the highway.

"Kayla left the diary for me to find. I'm positive now."

"Why?"

"Why else put the Pierce Bluejays emblem inside the diary? She knew I grew up there, and I'd pick up on the clue."

"But why not tell you what was happening?"

"Kayla might've been gathering information, and I was her fail-safe. Or, fearing someone was after her, she might've protected me."

That made sense. On the drive, they pondered the possibilities of what the safe-deposit box might hold. Trey pulled into the First Bank of Pierce parking lot at ten minutes before six o'clock. "Go on ahead of me. I'll get Magnum and meet you."

"Okay." Justine bolted from the truck and through the bank's glass doors.

By the time Trey and Magnum entered the building, Justine was talking with a customer service representative. A nameplate on the round marble desk read Rachel. She appeared apprehensive and Trey overheard her say, "I'm sorry, ma'am. I cannot give you access to someone else's account."

"But it's a murder investigation," Justine insisted.

Rachel looked at Trey, sizing him up. "You're the trooper working with Miss Stark?"

His uniform pretty much answered that question,

but he nodded. "Yes, ma'am. I apologize for our late intrusion, but we really need to get into the safe-deposit box. We believe there's information directly applicable to this case."

Rachel frowned. "I'm not supposed to open it for anyone but the party, unless she listed someone else."

Justine leaned over the counter, nearly touching noses with Rachel. "Could you check the file?" Impatience in her tone evident.

The bank employee sighed and typed something into the computer. "What did you say your name was?"

"Justine Stark."

"May I see identification?"

Justine rummaged in her purse, then produced her wallet and driver's license. Rachel inspected the IDs, taking longer than necessary before handing them back to Justine. "You're listed on the account. I remember this one. So strange. Kayla Nolan paid for the box with a note to release it to you when you came."

Justine turned to Trey, the confusion on her face no doubt mirroring his own surprise.

"Let me get the keys." Rachel stepped away from the desk, returning a few seconds later with a ring of them in hand. "Please follow me."

They fell into step behind the woman, walking to a back room. Black safe-deposit boxes lined the walls on all sides and a large table in the center provided a place to view the contents. Trey and Magnum moved aside as Rachel inserted a key. Justine then inserted the key from the diary.

He held his breath. Would this solve Kayla's murder?

Rachel pulled the box free from the vault and placed it on the table. "I apologize for rushing you, but we will be closing in ten minutes. I'll give you some privacy." She exited, shut the door softly behind her.

Trey stepped closer.

Justine opened the box, revealing a stack of folded papers, which she flattened on the table. "They're statements from an offshore account in the Bahamas." She pointed a finger at the name. "Underwood Machler is listed as the owner."

Trey leaned forward, reading beside Justine. "Wow, that's a lot of money."

"Why would Kayla have copies of bank records for this Machler?" She passed a set to Trey.

He scanned the documents, homing in on a line repeating several times each month. "Look, there are transactions from Nolan and Associates to this account."

Justine flipped through the rest of the papers. "These are invoices for business meetings and services, but there are no details listed and the contact for the company is Underwood Machler."

Trey glanced up. "What's the last date on the invoices?"

"July 26." Justine withdrew the diary and laid it on the table. "One week before Kayla's final entry."

"Who signed them?"

"Alex Duncan." Justine folded the papers. "This is fishy. There's an address on this account here in Nebraska."

"Let's go pay Mr. Machler a visit," Trey said.

"Should I assume you will not be needing the safe-deposit box anymore?" Rachel asked as they exited the room.

"No, ma'am. We'll take the contents."

"Very well."

Justine handed her the key and thanked Rachel for her help.

Once in the truck, Trey entered the address listed on the bank statements into his patrol GPS app and started the engine.

"I've never heard of this town," Justine said.

"It's in the middle of nowhere. GPS shows a two-hour drive from here."

"Let's get going."

"First, I need to make a call." Trey chose Slade's number.

"Hey, Will and I finished cleaning out the barn. The damage wasn't as bad as we thought," Slade said by way of greeting.

"That's great news. But I have a favor to ask."

"Aren't you out of those yet?"

"If this lead pans out, it'll be my last one." Trey gripped the steering wheel, anxious to get on the road.

"I'm listening, baby brother."

Trey sped through an explanation, hitting the high points and ending with the newfound information. "I'd like backup just in case. I have no idea what I'm walking into."

"Talk with Oliver first?"

"Not yet, but I will. Can you meet me out there?"

Slade sighed. "Yeah. I'll be on my way ASAP, but I'm more than two and a half hours away. Hang tight when you get close. We'll connect a mile out from the address and go in together."

"All right."

"Ask Oliver for backup," Slade repeated.

"But I don't know what I'm walking into. Could be absolutely nothing. And most likely he'd recommend Irwin again. I'm still not sure I trust him after the warehouse explosion," Trey confessed.

"I think the guy's good. A little obnoxious but not dirty. Promise you'll wait for me before you go charging into the place. And you'll give Oliver a heads-up."

Trey shook off the irritation at Slade's bossiness, conceding he was probably right. "I'll send you my location, and you can track me on the patrol app too."

"Roger that."

Trey typed a text to Oliver notifying him they'd be following up on a lead and he'd report in with an update ASAP, then shifted gears. "Now we're in business."

FOURTEEN

Trey parked in front of the decrepit structure and glanced at the dashboard clock. His phone had no service, and according to the patrol GPS app locator, Slade was running late. Dusk had settled in the valley, and they'd be hard-pressed to check out the old farmhouse before dark. Waiting on Slade wasn't an option.

Abandoned long ago, the neglected structure sagged on its crumbling frame. Dying trees with naked branches stretched out their limbs in a sad protectiveness around the home. Forest land bordered the property on every side, rising with the gentle rolling hills.

"Pretty," Justine quipped, one hand on the truck's door handle.

"Yeah. Think old Underwood Machler actually lives here?" Trey withdrew his weapon, checking the magazine.

"Um. No. But there might be clues to his actual location in there. Or the house will fall in on us while we're looking." Justine gave him a shaky smile.

Trey surveyed the property. "Maybe Machler used this address for the money laundering or whatever is going on. Wouldn't be the first time that's happened."

"True."

Trey put a hand on her arm. "Wait. Slade will be here soon. Stay inside the truck and lock the doors. I'll clear the house, and if it's empty, I'll come and get you. If I'm not back within three minutes, drive up to the hill, and as soon as you have reception, call Slade."

Justine shoved the diary into her pocket. "No way am I staying out here alone. Two eyes are better than one."

"In that case, I'll take Magnum with me. He's got two great eyeballs and a power sniffer."

On cue, Magnum popped his head through the divider, but Trey didn't miss the exhaustion in the animal's demeanor.

"Nice try. Not gonna happen. We're a team."

As much as he loved the sound of that, Trey made one last plea. "You do realize if something happens, we're too far from civilization to get help. The whole area is forest for miles."

"You're a terrible salesman."

He chuckled. "Sorry. Just giving you the facts."

"I appreciate the effort, but we're so close I can taste it."

Trey scratched Magnum's ear, concerned about the way he babied his injured paw. "Maybe I'll leave Magnum here."

"In a hot truck?"

"You forget the safety temperature controls." He gestured to the thermostat device between them.

"Right. Are you sure the windows will roll down?

And you've got that gadget to open his door if things go bad in there and we need Magnum?" Justine asked.

Trey pointed to a small black button on his vest, trying not to think of scenarios that might prohibit him from using the device. Like an ambush. "Yep, the engine stays running. Mags gets to chill in the AC, and we've got a quick getaway if needed."

"See? What do we have to lose?"

He turned up the air conditioner. "Mags, hang tight, buddy."

Magnum whined and slipped into his area. Trey slid the divider closed. Then they exited the truck, and he locked the doors.

"Follow me." Trey's pulse beat in his ears as they crept toward the house.

Thick air without a hint of a breeze had his shirt plastered to his back. Dead silence hedged about them, as if the elements held their breath.

Trey activated his weapon's flashlight, and they climbed the fragments of porch steps. Hypervigilance had him constantly surveying the area. "Stay close."

The comment was unnecessary since Justine was near enough he heard her breathing.

He gripped the rusty knob on the rickety door. Locked. Trey moved to the window and peered inside. It appeared abandoned. He returned to the front door and slammed his shoulder into the rotting wood, forcing it open. He scanned the threshold in search of any IED trip wires, then carefully crossed over, entering the living room. Only a moth-eaten sofa filled the space, and the floors creaked beneath his boots.

He quickly cleared the area and whispered, "Wait here."

Justine shook her head, and he shot her a pleading look. She conceded, moving farther into the room as he eased into the hallway and across to the kitchen.

"Trey!"

He spun, sweeping the flashlight beam off Susan's pistol, pressed to Justine's temple. Where had she come from?

"Drop your gun, or I'll shoot your girlfriend."

"Then I'd have to return fire," he countered. His mind raced. They'd diligently watched for anyone following them on the way and had seen no one for miles. How did Susan know they'd be here?

"You're wondering how we knew you'd show up." Susan's lip curved in a sneer.

We. Who was with her? "Something like that," Trey said, focused on the open front door and his pickup parked in the distance.

"You'd be amazed what information money will buy, Trooper." Susan laughed.

Gun unwavering, he slowly raised his left hand up to his tactical vest, to Magnum's emergency-door-release button.

"Put down your weapon!" Susan screeched.

"I wouldn't test her, Trooper." Alex's familiar

voice was accompanied by the jabbing of a gun barrel in Trey's back.

He dropped his hand. "Glad to see you manned up and came out of hiding, Alex. But you'll never get away with anything. There's a BOLO out for your arrest," Trey warned.

The sun had almost set, darkening the room.

"We? Is Underwood Machler here with you?" Justine's voice took on that professional sound.

Susan chuckled. "Some secrets are too precious."

"Secrets Kayla discovered," Justine said.

"If she'd minded her own business, she would've lived," Alex inserted.

"You killed her," Justine replied.

"He did what had to be done," Susan defended.

"Drop your gun and kick it to me." Alex pressed the gun harder.

"Don't do it, Trey," Justine cried.

"Say another word and I'll finish you off," Susan bit out, slamming the butt of her weapon against Justine's temple. She yelped and met his eyes, pleading.

Trey lunged forward, halted by a warning shot near Justine's foot.

"Drop your gun or the next bullet is for Justine," Alex warned, stepping closer.

"Okay, calm down." Trey glanced toward the door.

Justine's eyes widened with what he prayed was understanding. He sank to a squat, placed the gun

on the floor beside him and used the diversion to
depress Magnum's release button.

Barks resounded.

Alex cursed and shoved Trey down, stomping on
Trey's hand as he lunged, and slammed the door
shut before Magnum reached the porch.

Trey jumped to his feet and tackled Alex to the
ground. Alex's gun slid toward Trey.

Out of the corner of his eye, he saw Justine spin,
elbowing Susan in the nose.

Relentless, Magnum snarled, clawing and butt-
ing the door.

"It's over. Get up!" Trey ordered.

A warning shot rained bits of wood and plaster
on Trey, and he turned.

Justine knelt on one knee, a sliver of crimson
sliding down her face.

"It's far from over, Trooper." Susan shoved her
weapon against Justine's head. "Put your gun down
now, or I'll shoot her."

Magnum slammed against the door again, barking furiously. Without an injured paw, he'd easily jump through the window, but Trey prayed he
wouldn't try as he set down his pistol.

"Move to the couch," Alex ordered.

Trey complied. "So, you're Underwood Machler?"

"Oh, please. We're not going to have one of those
last-minute-revelation discussions."

"But even if you kill us, we have the evidence to
put you away," Trey stalled.

Alex sneered. "I doubt that. And by the time your cohorts figure out you two are missing, we'll be long gone, lounging in the Bahamas."

Magnum continued hitting the door and barking.

"Shut that dog up before I shoot him!" Susan raged.

Fury showed in Justine's eyes, locking with Trey's. A silent acknowledgment to fight.

"Too bad dogs can't open doors. I'll take care of the cop. Get what you need from Justine. And do whatever it takes," Alex ordered.

Susan dragged Justine down the hallway.

Alex stepped closer, kicking Trey's Glock under the couch.

Trey dived for the man's legs, tackling him with such vigor they went through the rotting floor and landed on the dirt below.

Alex lost his hold on the gun, but the attorney was more agile than Trey anticipated.

He kicked Trey back and scurried up from the ground.

Trey punched Alex, landing several uppercuts, but Alex hooked a foot around Trey's leg, tripping him.

Alex jumped on Trey, punches flying.

Trey dodged a jab and gained the top position. He drove a fist into Alex's stomach and ribs.

Alex clocked Trey, igniting fury.

With three quick hits, Trey pummeled Alex,

knocking him unconscious, and then got to his feet, stepping out of the hole.

Trey yanked open the door, and Magnum bolted inside, rushing to Alex and growling at the unresponsive man. "Good boy!"

Darkness had settled, and shadows covered the landscape. How would he find Justine?

Alex groaned, and Trey pulled him through the broken floor and slapped handcuffs over his wrists. He collected his gun from under the couch and grabbed Alex's weapon, then slid it into his waistband.

Magnum sniffed the room. He'd have to rely on the dog's ability to track Justine and Susan. They moved through the house and paused in the kitchen at the open back door. "Magnum, seek!"

The dog bolted outside, and Trey hurried after him. But Magnum sped over the ground and disappeared into the forest.

Please, Lord, let Magnum find Justine. They couldn't have gone far.

Trey ran, debating whether to call Magnum. He didn't want to alert Susan, but he'd lost sight of the dog.

As if on cue, familiar barks echoed.

Magnum had found them!

Hope surged through Trey, fueling his search.

The forest was thick, reaching high, with a canopy of branches and leaves blocking the moonlight.

Trey sprinted, arms outstretched to thwart the

low-hanging limbs slapping at him from all directions. There was no path to follow, and the ground was covered with brambles and exposed roots, forcing Trey to move slower.

Ears straining, he aimed toward Magnum's barks. The sound seemed to come from everywhere and inky night smothered him, confusing his sense of direction.

Trey paused, activated his weapon's flashlight and whistled a response.

A gunshot exploded.

Justine glanced down at the creek separating her from Magnum's scent trail. She'd heard him rushing through the leaves, but he hadn't reached her before Susan had forced her across the water. She prayed he'd lead Trey to where she'd dropped the diary and know they'd crossed over.

Susan grew more agitated, escalating her irrational behavior. Pain seared from the bullet-grazing wound of Susan's last warning shot.

"Why not kill me here?" Justine pressed.

"Walk!" Susan seethed, but something in her attitude hinted that things weren't going as planned.

Trey's whistle echoed, a comforting reminder he searched for her in the enveloping darkness, Magnum's barks promising to find her.

But would that happen before Susan killed her?

"I can't see where I'm going." Justine clumsily traversed the sloping ground.

"Shut up and walk."

Stumbling through the brambles, Justine determined to keep Susan talking. "Where are you taking me?" The leaves and pine needles crunched beneath their shoes.

"Where they won't find your body." The iciness in Susan's voice sent a shiver down Justine's back.

Magnum's barks faded. Was he going the wrong way?

Though her eyes had adjusted, she couldn't see two feet in front of her.

Lord, help them find me.

Her head throbbed from where Susan had struck her with the gun.

"Where is he?" Susan murmured, confirming Justine's suspicions Alex was the brains behind everything.

But why?

"Alex will give you up. He's already in custody," Justine surmised, praying she was right.

"You don't know anything." Susan's voice quavered.

"Don't let him get away with killing Kayla. I'll go in with you, explain how he manipulated you."

"Shut up! I need to think!"

Justine paused and turned.

Susan stood close behind her.

She was breaking down. Whatever plot she and Alex had was unraveling. Justine used her most soothing tone. "Susan, there's time to stop this.

I'll give you the diary. We can talk to the police together. You don't want another murder on your hands."

A streak of moonlight pierced through the trees overhead. A silent second ticked by and Susan faced her, a murderous glare lasered on Justine. "You think you're so smart, don't you?"

"If you surrender before Alex does, you'll have leverage."

"I'll be gone before that happens. Alex served his purpose."

The woman bounced between calculating to unsure. Had she been the one behind the psychological games against Kayla? Justine stepped closer, hands outstretched. "Susan, I want to help."

From the depths of the night, Magnum's barks grew stronger.

Susan turned, and Justine barreled into her.

They slammed into a tree.

Justine grasped the woman's gun-wielding arm.

"No!" Susan screeched, the weapon swaying dangerously above them in Susan's attempt to maintain control.

Justine thrust Susan's hand into the trunk, and Susan accidentally fired the gun a second time.

Like a beacon to their location, Magnum's barking drew closer.

"Magnum!" Justine held on tight, unwilling to release Susan's arm.

The woman kicked, striking Justine's injured leg.

Pain exploded, and she buckled but refused to let Susan go.

Fury infused Justine with adrenaline, and she straightened and headbutted Susan. The gun toppled to the ground, and the impact sent them both stumbling.

Magnum's barks ceased. Had he left?

Justine's vision clouded, but she couldn't stop. She swung hard, landing a blow to Susan's face.

Susan wasn't giving up easily. She lunged, tackling Justine, and pinned her down.

Susan swung wildly. Two strikes to her ribs stunned Justine as she fought to dodge the attacks.

She tucked her knees up, prepared to shove Susan off.

A blur of black appeared from the brush, and Susan flew to the side.

Justine bolted to her feet.

Magnum stood on guard, teeth bared, hackles raised.

"He will attack," Justine warned through painful breaths, though she wasn't sure he'd act on her command. Where was Trey?

Susan froze, braced on all fours, chest heaving with exertion.

"Justine!" A light bounced in the distance.

"Here!"

Trey sprinted through the dark, rushing to her side. He jerked Susan to her feet.

"Good boy, Magnum." Justine hugged him.

Susan huffed, hands cuffed behind her. "Wait. I'll give you a cut of the money."

"Forget it. Trey, can you hand me that flashlight?"

He swept his weapon light across the area. Justine pressed an arm against her ribs. "I can't find her gun."

"Magnum, evidence."

The dog scurried, nose to the ground, moving beside a thicket, then dropped to a sit. Trey shone the beam on Susan's weapon.

Justine eased out of her outer shirt and used it to pick up the gun.

Sirens blared in the distance.

"Oh, sure. Now big brother shows up," Trey teased, leading the group through the woods.

As they neared the creek, Justine asked, "Did you find the diary?"

Trey nodded. "Yep, got it in my pocket. Great idea, by the way."

Susan gaped but said nothing.

They hiked back to the house, using the strobing lights to guide the way. Entering the clearing, Justine exhaled relief at the two patrol cars parked beside Trey's pickup.

Eric Irwin hauled a swaying and stumbling Alex from the house.

Trey shot her a look.

"Be nice," she whispered.

He grunted.

"What happened to Alex?" Justine asked.

"He made the mistake of trying to keep me from you," Trey said.

She grinned, grateful he couldn't see the warmth radiating up her neck.

Slade rushed to their side and took custody of Susan. "Thank God. We didn't know where you'd disappeared to."

"You've got nothing on me. Alex forced me to do this. He's the mastermind," Susan ranted across the property.

"Lady, save it for your next attorney." Slade assisted her into his patrol car and closed the back door. He turned and faced Justine and Trey. "I'd ask why you didn't wait for me, but that seems to be a moot point."

"Sorry, but it all worked out." Trey grinned.

Slade snorted.

"Why'd you call him?" Trey jutted a chin at Eric, approaching from the side.

"You're welcome," Slade replied. "Instinct. I tracked your location and saw you'd ignored my suggestion and gone into the valley. I requested backup, and Irwin was the first to respond."

"I'm sure he was," Trey grumbled.

"Bro, he's cool."

Justine watched the interaction as Trey sized up the other trooper.

"Did you tell him?" Eric smiled wide.

"Tell me what?" Trey asked.

"Eric did a little background search on this property. Turns out it belonged to the Underwood family," Slade explained.

Justine and Trey exchanged glances.

"And?" Justine invaded the pregnant pause.

"And Underwood was Susan's maternal grandmother's name. She left the property to Susan, who 'sold'—" Eric made air quotes with his fingers "—it to Underwood Malcher. They made up the name, used a fake Social Security number and created a false identity."

"You discovered that tonight?" Justine queried.

Eric shrugged. "The internet is full of mystery. Besides, it's all a team effort, right?"

Trey ducked his head and held out a hand. "Outstanding work. I owe you."

Eric guffawed, shaking his hand. "I want that in writing."

"Alex and Susan embezzled money from the Nolans' business into the offshore account. When Kayla found out, she made the copies of the documents," Justine clarified.

"And they killed her before she ratted them out," Trey finished. "But how do we prove who actually injected Kayla with the drugs?"

Slade laughed. "Alex is rambling like a babbling two-year-old. He flat out admitted he didn't mean to kill Kayla. He'll turn on Susan in a heartbeat."

"The dream team stole the show." Eric beamed, slapping Trey on the back a little harder than necessary, based on the accompanying wince.

Justine stifled a giggle.

"Unless you want the honors of booking Alex, I'll take him in," Eric offered.

"He's all yours," Trey said.

"Fantastic." Eric jogged to his patrol car.

"Hey, Eric?" Trey called.

He turned.

"Hold off a few minutes."

"Roger that." Eric saluted and resumed walking to his vehicle.

"See?" Slade put a hand on Trey's shoulder.

"I really had him pegged as a vulture," Trey admitted.

"Nah, bro, he's just young and eager. Can't blame a guy for wanting to jump in and swim." Slade fist-bumped his brother, then turned to Justine. "Will's doing an amazing job at the ranch. You'll be able to sleep in your house tonight."

Justine covered her arms with her hands, suddenly self-conscious of the exposed burn scars and grateful for the dark atmosphere. "Thank you, Slade, for everything."

"That's what family does." He grinned.

"I want to talk to Alex while he's still chatty," Trey said.

"I'll meet you at Booking so you can wrap up here." Slade rounded his patrol car and slid behind the wheel.

Trey and Justine walked to Eric. He opened the back door to where Alex sat.

"She made me. I tried to talk Susan out of it all, but she insisted. What else could I do?" The hope in Alex's eyes was almost comical.

"Let's skip the part where you deny any knowledge of this whole situation," Trey said.

Alex slumped in the seat. "All Kayla had to do was leave it alone. Susan said we'd just scare her. Use the stalker thing to get Kayla off the trail and make her look unstable."

"You used terror to control her, but it didn't work. Kayla was too strong for you," Justine said.

Alex blinked. "I really did like Kayla, but she locked us out of the Underwood account. That sent Susan over the edge."

"So all this time, you haven't been able to get to the money?" Justine asked.

Alex nodded. "Then, when you called about the diary, we figured she'd hidden the information in it. If you'd just given it back, none of this would've happened."

"You're not seriously blaming me?" Justine gaped at the man.

He shrugged. "No one had to die."

"Who injected Kayla?" Justine pressed.

"If I tell you, will you cut me a deal?"

"You watch too many crime-TV shows." Trey shook his head and reached for the door.

"Wait! There's more! Susan set that IED at the warehouse. I wasn't even there."

Justine leaned against the quarter panel. "Except you were."

"No. I wasn't. Honest."

"Prove it," Trey said.

"Sure! How?"

"Let me see your leg."

Alex's eyes widened. "Why? What's that got to do with anything?"

Magnum sat beside Justine with that knowing smile of his.

"I can get a warrant, but we both know what I'm going to find," Trey said.

Alex shifted, placing his leg on the outer edge of the door. "Stupid dog."

Eric leaned in. "Now, Apollo won't like that kind of attitude," he said, pointing to the dog's kenneled area beside Alex.

The man paled.

Trey lifted Alex's pant leg. A bite mark on his calf screamed the truth. "Magnum, is that your handiwork?"

The dog wagged his tail.

Alex tucked his leg in the truck.

"Thanks, Alex. I'll see you in Booking." Trey grinned.

"Got what you wanted?" Eric asked.

"Yep. Meet you at the office." Trey slammed the door and Alex startled.

Eric exited the property, Slade behind him.

Justine giggled. "Thank you."

"For what?"

"For showing up at the perfect time. Susan might've killed me."

"Nah, you had her."

She grinned and leaned over, inspecting her leg.

"You're hurt!" Trey squatted beside her.

"It hurts worse than it looks," she teased.

Trey lifted her and carried Justine to his pickup. Setting her down, he pulled out a first-aid kit and cleaned the wound.

"Nice." Justine inspected the bandage.

"Still need to see the doctor."

She smiled. "Magnum's rescue more than proves he's K-9 material. The bite is solid evidence against Alex."

"He did a great job, didn't ya, buddy?" Trey ruffled Magnum's mane. "Too bad that doesn't count for the recertification."

"He's earned a little R & R. Let's see how he does after that."

Trey shrugged. "The funny thing is, I'm okay with whatever happens. I can train a new dog, and Eric deserves to work Apollo. Regardless, Mags is my partner, and even if he's forced to retire, he's staying with me."

"I love the way you think."

Trey chuckled. "See, that optimism of yours totally wore off on me. It's one of the many things I love about you."

Justine blinked. Her mouth went dry, and she

rubbed her arms, longing for her long-sleeved shirt to cover the scars.

Trey covered her hands with his. "I love you, Justine. If you feel the same, I'll wait a year, ten years, whatever it takes, but I want to be with you. Forever. You've always been the one."

His words burst through the floodgates of her heart, and Justine melted into his embrace. Had she hidden behind Kayla because she feared falling for Trey? Would Kayla approve? Justine tipped back, her gaze meeting Trey's.

Yes, her friend had known how Trey felt. It was time to release the past.

Justine leaned in.

Trey's mouth parted, and she paused, their lips a breath apart. She whispered, "I love you too," and initiated a kiss.

This time, the connection was no longer tentative.

But deepened with acceptance and promise for their future.

EPILOGUE

The stifling summer heat was unbearable, but Justine wouldn't be anywhere else. She stood at a distance, watching as Trey and Magnum worked through the recertification exercises.

Anxiety oozed through her and she transitioned from biting her fingernails to worrying her lip, whispering, "Come on."

They'd babied Magnum for the past two weeks, just for this day.

Eric, Sergeant Oliver and Slade stood to one side of Justine, Will on the other. As Magnum and Trey completed each section, the group shouted, "Yes!" and exchanged fist bumps.

But their enthusiasm didn't compare to the boisterous Jackson clan, cheering behind them.

"One short break, then the final test," Slade explained.

"They're an amazing team." She glanced up to see Fredrick Nolan approaching. "Hi there. What're you doing here?"

"I heard this is where you and Trooper Jackson were today."

"We'll give you some privacy." Eric ushered Slade toward the Jackson group and said, "Introduce me to your younger sister."

"No way." Slade laughed, shaking his head.

Fredrick gazed out at the course. "I wanted to say thank-you."

"I'm glad everything worked out."

"Took a little bit for me to accept Susan and Alex betrayed me. Worse, I didn't want to believe they were responsible for Kayla's death."

Justine faced him, compassion warming her heart. "I'm so sorry."

"My new attorney says Susan will be forced to repay the life insurance money."

"The Slayer Rule," Justine interpreted.

"Such an appropriate name for it, don't you think?" Sadness filled Fredrick's eyes. "The money was withdrawn in cash portions, making it untraceable. We're guessing she used it to pay off those she'd recruited to support her quest to stop Kayla and the investigation."

Though Justine and Trey suspected Laslo Drazin was one of those people, there was no paper trail to prove it.

"But that's not why I came. Kayla loved life. She wanted everyone to be happy and joyful. She brought sparkle to everything she did. I miss that most about her."

Justine nodded, emotion thickening her throat.

"She would be happy for you and Trooper Jackson."

Justine startled. "Beg your pardon?"

"Miss Stark, I'm an old man but not a blind one.

Trooper Jackson is in love with you. Don't waste a second denying your heart."

Tears filled Justine's eyes at the familiar saying. "Kayla said that all the time."

"Yes, she did. And it was good advice." He winked. "I also came to deliver this." He passed an envelope to Justine.

She startled at the whistle. "They're beginning again." They focused on Trey and Magnum's final part of the course.

The pair eased through the last portion, finishing before the allotted time.

"They did it!" Justine jumped to her feet.

Raucous yelling from the Jackson crew drowned out her cheers, and Fredrick laughed.

Trey stopped to praise Magnum and rushed to Justine. "We're back in the game!"

"Outstanding!" Justine lunged into his arms. Then, remembering Fredrick beside her, she released her hold. "Look who came to support you."

"Mr. Nolan, it's good to see you."

"Fredrick, please." He knelt and petted Magnum. "You all were amazing out there."

"It's all Magnum. I just hold the leash." Trey beamed.

"He is a beautiful creature."

Magnum did the adorable smile that tugged at Justine's heart. She looked down at the envelope. "Fredrick brought this."

"Yes, please open it."

Justine unsealed the envelope and gasped at the amount written on the first check made out to the victims' advocacy center. "Sir, this is very generous."

Fredrick bowed his head, hands in his pants pockets. "I can't bring back my daughter, but I can help others in her memory so women facing stalkers or trouble might have the resources they need. The resources I should've encouraged Kayla to take part in."

"I'm sure they'll be very grateful," Trey said.

Tears filled Justine's eyes.

She froze at the sight of the second check made out to her. "Sir. I can't. It's too much. I can't—"

Fredrick lifted a hand. "Miss Stark, after Trooper Jackson told me about Susan and Alex's horrendous efforts to silence you and the extensive damage they caused your ranch, I could not turn a blind eye. Please accept the money. In Kayla's memory. I'd be hurt if you refused."

Justine nodded and bit her quivering lip. "Thank you."

He grinned brightly. "You all have a good day." He turned and walked away, happiness in his step.

"The suspense is killing me," Trey said.

Justine showed him the check, and his eyes widened. "I've never seen that many zeros before a decimal point."

"It's more than enough to fix my house, the barn and pay Will two years' full-time salary!"

Trey pulled her into his arms. "That's fantastic. Now that Mags and I are finished with the recert, I have one important thing to take care of."

"Oh, yeah? What's that?"

Trey released his hold and withdrew a box from his tactical vest.

Justine gasped as he opened it to reveal an antique diamond ring.

"It was my great-grandmother's. She and my great-grandfather were married seventy years." He dropped to a knee and everything went silent around Justine. "Would you do me the honor of becoming my wife?"

Justine couldn't speak over the lump in her throat, so she nodded her head vigorously instead.

"Is that a yes?" one of his sisters called from behind them.

"Yes!" Justine finally found her voice.

Trey embraced her and she melted into him.

Whoops and hollers cut the kiss short as the Jackson clan, Will, Sergeant Oliver and Eric surrounded them, enfolding Trey and Justine into the family she'd always longed for.

* * * * *

Dear Reader,

Thank you for sharing in Trey, Justine and Magnum's story. I find K-9s fascinating and I am always amazed at their abilities. My own German shepherd doesn't have Magnum's skill set, and he's no K-9, but like Magnum, he definitely has a personality all his own. I'm positive he smiles too.

Characters often teach me as they come to life on the pages of a book. That's certainly true of Justine. She's an overcomer, determined to make a difference for the better even after everything she's been through.

Many of us face hardships, suffering and pain. But it's what we choose to do with that pain that offers hope in a hurting world. I am reminded of 2 Corinthians 1:3–5, which tells us to comfort one another with the same comfort God has shown us. Your story of endurance might be what someone else needs to hear today so they know they can get through it too.

Know that God sees you. He loves you. And He doesn't waste a single tear.

I love hearing from my readers, so let's stay in touch. Please join my newsletter at www.shareestover.com.

Blessings to you,
Sharee

Get 4 FREE REWARDS!

We'll send you 2 FREE Books plus 2 FREE Mystery Gifts.

Love Inspired books feature uplifting stories where faith helps guide you through life's challenges and discover the promise of a new beginning.

FREE
Value Over
$20

YES! Please send me 2 FREE Love Inspired Romance novels and my 2 FREE mystery gifts (gifts are worth about $10 retail). After receiving them, if I don't wish to receive any more books, I can return the shipping statement marked "cancel." If I don't cancel, I will receive 6 brand-new novels every month and be billed just $5.24 each for the regular-print edition or $5.99 each for the larger-print edition in the U.S., or $5.74 each for the regular-print edition or $6.24 each for the larger-print edition in Canada. That's a savings of at least 13% off the cover price. It's quite a bargain! Shipping and handling is just 50¢ per book in the U.S. and $1.25 per book in Canada.* I understand that accepting the 2 free books and gifts places me under no obligation to buy anything. I can always return a shipment and cancel at any time. The free books and gifts are mine to keep no matter what I decide.

Choose one: ☐ **Love Inspired Romance**
                    Regular-Print
                    (105/305 IDN GNWC)

☐ **Love Inspired Romance**
  Larger-Print
  (122/322 IDN GNWC)

Name (please print)

Address   Apt. #

City   State/Province   Zip/Postal Code

Email: Please check this box ☐ if you would like to receive newsletters and promotional emails from Harlequin Enterprises ULC and its affiliates. You can unsubscribe anytime.

Mail to the **Harlequin Reader Service:**
IN U.S.A.: P.O. Box 1341, Buffalo, NY 14240-8531
IN CANADA: P.O. Box 603, Fort Erie, Ontario L2A 5X3

Want to try 2 free books from another series? Call 1-800-873-8635 or visit www.ReaderService.com.

Get 4 FREE REWARDS!

We'll send you 2 FREE Books plus 2 FREE Mystery Gifts.

Harlequin Heartwarming Larger-Print books will connect you to uplifting stories where the bonds of friendship, family and community unite.

FREE Value Over $20

YES! Please send me 2 FREE Harlequin Heartwarming Larger-Print novels and my 2 FREE mystery gifts (gifts worth about $10 retail). After receiving them, if I don't wish to receive any more books, I can return the shipping statement marked "cancel." If I don't cancel, I will receive 4 brand-new larger-print novels every month and be billed just $5.74 per book in the U.S. or $6.24 per book in Canada. That's a savings of at least 21% off the cover price. It's quite a bargain! Shipping and handling is just 50¢ per book in the U.S. and $1.25 per book in Canada.* I understand that accepting the 2 free books and gifts places me under no obligation to buy anything. I can always return a shipment and cancel at any time. The free books and gifts are mine to keep no matter what I decide.

161/361 HDN GNPZ

Name (please print)

Address   Apt. #

City   State/Province   Zip/Postal Code

Email: Please check this box ☐ if you would like to receive newsletters and promotional emails from Harlequin Enterprises ULC and its affiliates. You can unsubscribe anytime.

> ### Mail to the **Harlequin Reader Service:**
> **IN U.S.A.:** P.O. Box 1341, Buffalo, NY 14240-8531
> **IN CANADA:** P.O. Box 603, Fort Erie, Ontario L2A 5X3

Want to try 2 free books from another series! Call 1-800-873-8635 or visit www.ReaderService.com.

---

*Terms and prices subject to change without notice. Prices do not include sales taxes, which will be charged (if applicable) based on your state or country of residence. Canadian residents will be charged applicable taxes. Offer not valid in Quebec. This offer is limited to one order per household. Books received may not be as shown. Not valid for current subscribers to Harlequin Heartwarming Larger-Print books. All orders subject to approval. Credit or debit balances in a customer's account(s) may be offset by any other outstanding balance owed by or to the customer. Please allow 4 to 6 weeks for delivery. Offer available while quantities last.

Your Privacy—Your information is being collected by Harlequin Enterprises ULC, operating as Harlequin Reader Service. For a complete summary of the information we collect, how we use this information and to whom it is disclosed, please visit our privacy notice located at corporate.harlequin.com/privacy-notice. From time to time we may also exchange your personal information with reputable third parties. If you wish to opt out of this sharing of your personal information, please visit readerservice.com/consumerschoice or call 1-800-873-8635. **Notice to California Residents**—Under California law, you have specific rights to control and access your data. For more information on these rights and how to exercise them, visit corporate.harlequin.com/california-privacy.

HW21R

HARLEQUIN SELECTS COLLECTION

19 FREE BOOKS IN ALL!

From Robyn Carr to RaeAnne Thayne to Linda Lael Miller and Sherryl Woods we promise (actually, GUARANTEE!) each author in the Harlequin Selects collection has seen their name on the *New York Times* or *USA TODAY* bestseller lists!

YES! Please send me the **Harlequin Selects Collection**. This collection begins with 3 FREE books and 2 FREE gifts in the first shipment. Along with my 3 free books, I'll also get 4 more books from the Harlequin Selects Collection, which I may either return and owe nothing or keep for the low price of $24.14 U.S./$28.82 CAN. each plus $2.99 U.S./$7.49 CAN. for shipping and handling per shipment*.If I decide to continue, I will get 6 or 7 more books (about once a month for 7 months) but will only need to pay for 4. That means 2 or 3 books in every shipment will be FREE! If I decide to keep the entire collection, I'll have paid for only 32 books because 19 were FREE! I understand that accepting the 3 free books and gifts places me under no obligation to buy anything. I can always return a shipment and cancel at any time. My free books and gifts are mine to keep no matter what I decide.

☐ 262 HCN 5576   ☐ 462 HCN 5576

Name (please print)

Address   Apt. #

City   State/Province   Zip/Postal Code

Mail to the **Harlequin Reader Service:**
IN U.S.A.: P.O. Box 1341, Buffalo, NY 14240-8531
IN CANADA: P.O. Box 603, Fort Erie, Ontario L2A 5X3

---

*Terms and prices subject to change without notice. Prices do not include sales taxes, which will be charged (if applicable) based on your state or country of residence. Canadian residents will be charged applicable taxes. Offer not valid in Quebec. All orders subject to approval. Credit or debit balances in a customer's account(s) may be offset by any other outstanding balance owed by or to the customer. Please allow 3 to 4 weeks for delivery. Offer available while quantities last. © 2020 Harlequin Enterprises ULC. ® and ™ are trademarks owned by Harlequin Enterprises ULC.

Your Privacy—Your information is being collected by Harlequin Enterprises ULC, operating as Harlequin Reader Service. To see how we collect and use this information visit https://corporate.harlequin.com/privacy-policy. From time to time we may also exchange your personal information with reputable third parties. If you wish to opt out of this sharing of your personal information, please visit www.readerservice.com/consumerschoice or call 1-800-873-8635. Notice to California Residents—Under California law, you have specific rights to control and access your data. For more information visit https://corporate.harlequin.com/california-privacy.

50BOOKHS22R